Devious Intent

February 2, 2007

Devious Intent

Best of luck to Marli and Shel on their new home.
love Dad,

E Hinz

Edward Hinz

To order additional copies of this book, contact:
Xlibris Corporation
1-888-795-4274
www.Xlibris.com
Orders@Xlibris.com
37500

Dedication

I dedicate this book to my wife Mary and thank her for her patience and help during the many hours I devoted to writing.

Chapter 1

At the end of the workday, Teresa McCormick changed into her traveling clothes minus the hair rollers and scarf, in a reversal of her morning routine. She merged with the crowd headed for the subway entrance. Homeward bound people jammed the narrow platform. Teresa did not anticipate spending another evening in the Lower East Side apartment, shared with her widowed mother and aunt.

As she neared her rent-controlled building, the 'Welcome home' aroma of ethnic dinners filled the air. Young children, played handball, hopscotch and jump rope on the sidewalk; the teens gathered in groups. The reflection of the setting sun on the windows sparkled like jewels evenly set in the red brick buildings. The beauty of the moment ended when she entered the darkness of the foyer. She walked up the stairs for the exercise and to avoid the odor of urine in the graffiti decorated elevator. The stairwells were slight improvement.

At the fifth floor hallway, she heard her mother and aunt shouting in a mixed English and Cuban dialect. The closed door failed to muffle their shrill voices. She unlocked the door and walked through a long hallway toward the furor in the kitchen. Her estranged husband Frank, his face the color of his flame-red beard, confronted the women. They demanded he leave but he insisted on waiting for Teresa.

Separated for five years, Teresa thought she had seen the last of him. Her pulse raced. "How dare you come here? Get out! Get out-now!" she screamed.

"Why do you treat me so badly? I love you! Listen to me—a minute—please? These two old witches never liked me. I can't stand them—always chattering in a language that I can't understand."

Calling her mother and aunt old witches didn't help. Teresa's eyes blazed. "I don't love you, so forget it. I want a divorce! Why didn't you sign the papers my lawyer served you? I can't stand you—can't bear your touch—that will NEVER change!"

With hopes for reconciliation dashed, his ruddy complexion deepened on the verge of a stroke. "Catholics can't divorce! I need you! I'll never divorce you!"

In that moment, Teresa could kill him. Her nostrils flared. "Get out of here! NOW!" She grabbed her aunt's walking cane from the umbrella stand and struck Frank with all her strength. With his arms up to ward off the blows, he howled with pain. "What're you nuts?"

She continued the attack—the two women screamed. Frank, out-numbered and out-shouted, fearful of Theresa's wrath, ran out the door. At the end of the hallway, he turned, cupped his hands to his mouth, and shouted; his parting words echoed, "I'LL NEVER DIVORCE YOU!"

Breathless and temper out of-control, she searched the room for a heavy object—*the throw rug would do.* Her apartment overlooked the building entrance. She rolled the rug tight and tied it with a Venetian blind cord. She leaned precariously out the window holding the heavy cylindrical rug. He appeared—five stories below. She couldn't mistake his red beard and flaming hair. She took aim, adjusted for his gait and released the rug. It landed at his feet. *Damn, I missed!* From the open window, she watched him shrug his shoulders and walk out of sight. She ran down the stairs to retrieve the rug before another tenant appropriated it.

She wished he would disappear from her life. Since he refused to divorce her, she desperately needed a plan. Another emotional outburst could land her in jail.

*   *   *

Frank had his chances with women. The law of averages favored him based on the number of drinking establishments he frequented. After Teresa, no woman satisfied his desires. He missed her wild, uninhibited, passion. She spoiled him for all women.

Frank's muscular arms and firm torso, his Viking-red beard and matching thick hair lured various adventurous females to his bed. On these occasions, he remained sober, not venturing a single drink. At the decisive moment, he suffered an erectile failure. In total humiliation and with no explanation, he retreated into another room, dressed and quietly left his apartment. His lover in the height of passion, waited in vain. He silently cursed Teresa on these occurrences, and drowned his humiliation in drink. Sober, the memory of Teresa caused his impotence; inebriated, the alcohol . . . . He lived in a private limbo, stripped of his manhood. He blamed Teresa.

Disappointed at his failure to reconcile, Frank entered a bar at the arches that formed Brooklyn Bridge. After ordering a frothy stein of draft beer to cool his temper, he muttered, ". . . should have joined the priesthood—made my mother happy—to hell with Teresa—to hell with all women—screw 'em!.'" At that moment, a blond emanating whiskey and cheap perfume brushed her unbound breast against his arm—her timing bad. Frank snarled, "And that goes for you too. Beat it, whore!" She withdrew, indignant, saying to no one in particular, "What's eating him. The old fool!"

Five years earlier when Frank discovered Teresa's unfaithfulness, he came to this same tavern with the long dark walnut bar—varnish worn thin by countless elbows—the highly polished brass foot rest flanked by strategically placed spittoons—frozen in time—as Frank's life.

Frank went to Teresa's apartment that evening hopeful of reconciliation. His failure at love degraded him as a man. He loved Teresa and she hated him; he despised her effect on him. Her rejection was the supreme humiliation in his meaningless life. Frank drank until his numbed brain banished her from his thoughts. Inebriated, he staggered to the subway. He awoke in his Sunnyside apartment, with no memory of how he got there.

Chapter 2

Teresa glances around the office; her perfectionist boss, Phillip Noble, insists everything has its place. She arranges the mail on his desk by envelope size; he believes the smallest is most important. His frequent admonition, "Be organized!" irritates her. She cried often, until she learned to conform to his demands. *He thinks he can boss everybody—with his deep resonant voice, precise vocabulary, and persuasive manner. Not me! Yet, I shiver when his cold steel-gray eyes meet mine; they penetrate my soul. He fascinates, confuses and frustrates me. I hate him—hate him! Life would be simpler without him.* Nevertheless, Teresa dreams of a future with him—love, security, home, children, marriage—in any order.

Early that crisp sunny morning, her shadow raced before her on the gum-pocked Manhattan sidewalk as she walked from her East Village apartment to the Bleeker Street subway station. She rushed down the stairs and dangerously leaned over the platform's edge to see approaching lights of the #6 train. Doors parted and revealed a wall of human backs; despite warning signs, KEEP CLEAR OF DOORS, people leaned against them. She pushed her way into the ancient car and blended with the sleepy-eyed passengers. Doors closed and the train started with a lurch. Standees suspended from white enameled handles, swayed in unison with the train's motion. Teresa's height prevented sharing a handle. Besides, she did not savor the intimacy of the touch of a stranger's hand on her hand—an arm stretched over her shoulder—a body leaning against her—a stranger breathing upon her neck. She squirmed further into the car. She moved toward an empty seat but recoiled from the odor of wine and urine. A homeless man in his mid-fifties, with long matted beard, tangled hair, and layers of unwashed clothing, clasped an open bottle partially concealed by a brown paper bag. Slouched on the long seat, oblivious to the discomfort of his fellow riders, he slept. Sporadic snores overpowered the rhythmic sound of the speeding train. The crowd, held at bay by an invisible barrier, formed a discreet semi-circle. Teresa struggled to distance herself from him.

To keep her balance, she threaded her arm between a man and a woman and commandeered six inches of a vertical white pole. Swaying in unison, Teresa avoided contact with their clothing. She imagined parasites, lice, fleas, and possibly roaches eager to invade her person. At Grand Central Station, she pushed through the opening doors. On the platform, she stopped a moment; examined and adjusted her clothing before the crowd swept her through the gates, up the stairs into the sunlight. Teresa deeply inhaled the crisp autumn air unpolluted by the light traffic. The year 1974 brought muscle cars named Barracuda™, Challenger™, GTO™ and GTX™ equipped with 4-barrel carburetors and dual exhaust systems to increase horsepower and create by noon, a bluish haze over the city streets.

Teresa daydreamed as she joined the steady stream of silent people. *Someday, I will not need to work or suffer the indignities of a subway rider. My sleek black limousine with tinted glass will drive to the building entrance. A smartly uniformed chauffer will open the door and assist me for a graceful arrival.*

Thousands of shoes striking the cement sidewalk broke the eerie silence of workers headed toward building entrances, through lobbies and into elevators. Settled in office cubicles, their silence ended. Over the inevitable cup of coffee, they exchanged greetings and discussed where they dined and with whom, the popular TV program, "The Rockford Files™" with James Garner and Lindsay Wagner, and the news reports of charges against President Nixon that resulted in his resignation. Teresa, through habit, arrived early to prepare for Mr. Noble's arrival.

Although unattractive, her traveling ensemble was practical. She wore a flowered scarf covering several non-matching rollers in her hair, a gray all-weather topcoat, and battered white walking shoes with gray Nike® lettering. She placed her topcoat in her locker and reached for a virgin wool blue jacket, and then hurried to the rest room. She hung her jacket and washed away the subway grime. As she entered the stall, an acrid odor evoked a fleeting image of the homeless man. She sighed with relief after attending to urgent matters; she welcomed the cold water on her hands. With deft fingers, she unwound rollers from her auburn hair, and combed it into soft springy curls. She brushed a hint of blusher on her cheeks and with eyeliner accentuated her brown eyes. After penciling the outline of her lips, she applied a pale pink lipstick, pouted and smiled at the mirror, pleased with her reflection. She removed the ugly white cotton crew socks worn over white nylon stockings. Light blue high-heeled shoes, one of five pairs kept at the office, completed her makeover. She adjusted her white skirt upward to reveal her knees, then donned her jacket and stepped back to appraise her appearance in the mirror. *I hope Mr. Noble appreciates my efforts.*

As Teresa walked toward her desk, Alicia's strident "You're looking good." interrupted Teresa's thoughts.

"Thank you. Is Mr. Noble in?"

"No—he isn't." After hesitating a moment and aware of Teresa's interest in Mr. Noble, Alicia added, "He's married. Leave him alone. Besides, you have a husband—Frank—or have you forgotten?"

Teresa piqued at Alicia's reference to the man absent for five years responded, "You're jealous! Get a life!" Alicia feared the end of their friendship.

Alicia headed the office rumor mill. She derived vicarious pleasure and interest in office romances. Her inability to attract a man caused an anxiety disorder diagnosed as hyperhydrosis, profuse sweating at inopportune moments. The office air-conditioning failed to prevent beads of perspiration on her forehead, neck and cleavage. By day's end, she permeated the air with deodorant mixed with cologne. Alicia envied Teresa's fresh, cool and confident appearance. Before Teresa's assignment as Mr. Noble's assistant, Alicia frequently joined her for lunch in the cafeteria. Teresa deliberately discussed her conquests, taking pleasure in Alicia's prurient interest.

During a recent luncheon conversation, Teresa provided explicit details about her affair with Tom from the mailroom—how she targeted and manipulated him. Alicia admired Tom—tall, strong and virile, in his mid-twenties with long blond hair tied in back to appear less conspicuous at work. Teresa described his unbound hair brushing her bare breasts during intimacy—and their response. Anticipating every word, Alicia perspired. With her handkerchief, she mopped her neck and forehead as Teresa described their entwined bodies and passionate climax. Luncheon over, flustered and damp, Alicia could not recall what she ate—only that her dearest friend shared most intimate secrets.

Teresa's obsessive behavior frightened Tom; although he enjoyed the furtive torrid sex, she demanded more than he could give. With exercise and healthy diet, she maintained her body in peak physical condition. Although she was wild and uninhibited, he avoided her. A mutual understanding parted them. Against her nature, she chose celibacy—she would settle for none other than Phil Noble.

As Mr. Noble entered the office, to appear busy she picked up the appointment book. He hesitated at her desk. She did not look up; she waited for him to speak.

"Good morning, Teresa. What's on for today?"

She was inclined to answer, "I am." Instead, as her eyes met his, she smiled—her pink lips in contrast with her perfect white teeth. "Good morning, Mr. Noble. Two documents require immediate attention." *I require your immediate attention.*

"Give me ten minutes."

Her fingers tapped on the desk in synch with the second hand on the clock. She lived for time with Phil. When she gave him an envelope or document, she trembled as their hands touched. If she saw him walk toward the elevator, she timed her activities, to enter with him, stand close, accidentally brush against him and grasp his arm when the elevator lurched. She contrived any excuse for contact.

When Teresa bought perfume for his wife's birthday, she asked the sales girl for samples. Engrossed in Business Week© he neglected to look at her as she placed the papers on his desk; she knew he recognized the fragrance. Seated far enough to provide an unobstructed view, she waited with legs crossed. She arranged her skirt to reveal the underside of her thigh with a bit of pale skin exposed above her white hosiery—disappointed that he failed to respond.

She studied the framed picture of Phil and his wife, Margaret, happy together on Bermuda's pink sand. Taken on their vacation last August, the photo could have been a travel advertisement. Bikini swimwear provided scant cover for their bronzed bodies. Her thoughts wandered. *If only I could replace Margaret's image with mine. Nestle my shoulder under his arm; feel the tickle of his hairy armpit and the combined moisture of our skin cooled by Bermudan breezes.*

Immersed in fantasy, she dropped her pen at the sound of his voice. "My, you look attractive this morning." She was ecstatic. "That will be all . . . ." signaled the end of their brief meeting. Teresa flashed a winning smile in his direction, and sensed his eyes following her as she reluctantly departed with sensuous thoughts provoked by the photo and his presence. *How can I tell him what I feel? I would love him—anytime—anywhere. Why does he act so proper—so married?*

*   *   *.

"Teresa? May I speak to my husband?" Teresa recognized the voice and lied. "I'm sorry. He's in conference. He instructed me not to interrupt him under any conditions."

"What time will the conference end?"

"Probably 1:00 . . . ."

"Please tell him I will meet him for lunch. It's important."

"I'll give him your message."

If Margaret mentions the conference, He'll know I lied. Will he ever trust me? I did it this time. Phil stepped from his office; "I'm meeting with Mr. Veidell and should return by noon." Teresa sighed, relieved. *Saved! Why did Margaret travel into Manhattan?*

*   *   *

Exquisite with long strawberry blond hair, flawless complexion and carrying two Bergdof Goodman™ bags, Margaret appeared the movie star. A silver fox half-coat covered a light gray pin-stripe jacket and silken white blouse. A diamond heart, framed by the 'V' of her neckline, swayed on a white-gold chain. Diamond cluster earrings peeked through strands of flowing hair. Jealousy overwhelmed Teresa. *Margaret has everything; the silver fox, shopping at Bergdof Goodman™, the diamond heart and earrings—all would be mine, if I were married to Phil.*

Teresa averted her face, unable to watch as Margaret embraced Phil and kissed him on the cheek. After their departure, a peculiar loneliness settled upon Teresa. *In the office, I spend many hours with Phil. Here he belongs to me, not Margaret.*

*   *   *

Phil stepped off the curb to hail a taxi. He opened the door and assisted Margaret, then entered from the street side before giving directions to the driver. The well-worn seat provided little support; he felt the hard metal through the vinyl covering. The hollowed out center brought them close together. The driver coaxed his vehicle around the ever-present construction cones, barricades, and double-parked delivery trucks, striking potholes without regard for the comfort of his passengers, while shouting foreign phrases aimed at the driving skills of his peers. His barbs combined with the noise of Manhattan traffic, made conversation impossible. Margaret snuggled close; Phil held her hand. The cab came to a halt, caught in a Manhattan traffic jam.

Phil, exulting in her beauty and subtle fragrance, studied Margaret. His thoughts wandered to the evening they met. He and his brother, Eric, ordered burgers and fries at the McDonald's™ drive-up window. As Margaret and her friend, Jo Ann, left the restaurant, Eric nudged Phil. Phil choked on his drink. "What a knockout!" He called out, "Do you girls live around here?" A dozen clever introductory pickup lines filled his head, too late to withdraw his lame approach. Surprised that Margaret looked in his direction, he ventured, "Would you consider dinner, other than here, tomorrow night?"

She hesitated and approached the car. He appeared sincere. "I appreciate the invitation—but no. I'm seeing someone."

"Then why aren't you with him, instead of your friend?"

"He's in Florida assigned to a Coast Guard Rescue Unit."

"But I'm here now. You're not engaged—are you?"

"No."

"Then what's the big deal?"

He insisted on dinner Friday night. Competition sharpened his interest and determination. He persevered until he obtained her phone number.

While Phil reminisced, Margaret thought of events that led her to their marriage. She recalled her teen years—her high school prom—the excitement shopping for the perfect gown—the first time a professional styled her long hair and the tears of disappointment at the results. She hurried home to mother.

"Look what they did to my hair!" I can't go to the prom."

"Let's see what we can do."

"It's a total mess."

"Hold still."

Mother successfully redid the hairstyle to Margaret's satisfaction.

A friend arranged her first real date with blonde, athletic Steve. During dinner, Margaret, spellbound by his azure blue eyes, listened attentively to tales of rescues off the Florida coast. After disco dancing, they ended the evening with a lingering goodnight kiss. Upon his return to duty, she wrote Steve daily for three months—until she met Phil.

Bubbling with excitement, she awakened her parents. "I met someone tonight. you'll like him. He's intelligent, well mannered and a perfect gentleman. Phil invited me for dinner Friday night. Wait until you meet him, Mom." She gushed on about the way they met. When she left the room, she heard Mom, "I think our little girl is in love."

Letters to Steve dwindled; she had written about feelings that existed only in her imagination. Now, she felt guilty dating Phil. They dined at exotic restaurants; enjoyed dancing and romantic walks on the boardwalk at Jones Beach. Phil often surprised her with gifts and flowers. Steve faded into distant memory.

One evening, while dining, Phil opened a tiny white velvet box. "For you." She marveled at the marquis diamond. ". . . to match the sparkle in your eyes. I never felt like this. I love you. Will you marry me?" Surprised, she quickly responded, "I love you too—yes I'll marry you." Phil placed the ring on her finger. Good-bye Steve.

Home on leave, Steve phoned. Against mother's advice, Margaret kept her engagement secret from him. She asked, "Mom, can Steve come to dinner tonight?" When Steve appeared promptly at six with a bouquet of flowers, she offered her cheek to kiss.

"You're sweet to bring flowers for my mother."

Bewildered, Steve awkwardly held the flowers while she casually inquired about his trip. Steve, flustered, gave mother the bouquet. Margaret nervously positioned her ring with the diamond facing her palm. At dinner, Margaret, seated next to Steve, held her fork with her right hand while her left hand rested on her lap. Assailed by her parent's meaningful looks, (When are you going to tell him?), Margaret averted her eyes. Stinted small talk added to her discomfort. Steve complimented Mom's cooking and thanked her. He turned to Margaret and asked her to accompany him for a walk. Outside, he held her hand, suspecting the worse when he discovered the ring. "What is going on? You've changed!"

Margaret confessed, "I met someone. I wanted to tell you in person."

"Bad news?"

"Yes—I'm sorry Steve."

"I'm sorry too."

He left her to walk home alone.

*   *   *

Liberated from the traffic jam, the taxi continued to Le Coquilles. Phil paid the fare with a generous tip that made the driver's bearded face crack a half-hidden smile. With an effusive greeting, the door attendant escorted them to the restaurant. Phil ignored the extended hand to the man's evident disappointment.

The luncheon crowd filled Le Coquilles; a line waited for tables. The *maitre d'*, Pierre, recognized Phil and whisked them through the archway separating the foyer and dining area. "Would you like a window table, Monsieur?"

Margaret replied, "I'd prefer one with privacy." She abhorred strangers peering at her meal. Besides, she hated to talk above the din of the main dining area. While Pierre led the way, she heard the rhythm of many languages in the cultural mix that is Manhattan. Pierre led them to a linen-covered table in an alcove surrounded by plastic plants, polished in a vain attempt to simulate a garden. With a practiced smile, Pierre asked, "Is this satisfactory, Madame?"

"Thank you."

He deftly held the chair for her. "Would Monsieur like the wine list?" Margaret interrupted, "I'll have Perrier, Pierre." Chuckling at Margaret's play on words, and Pierre's frown, Phil said. "And I'll have your best Chardonnay, please."

To Margaret he said, "Why the unexpected visit? You didn't come to shop. And when did you decline fine wine in favor of mineral water?"

"Since I learned I'm pregnant."

"How long have you known?"

"I'm in my seventh week. I needed to be sure before I told you."

"Our whole lifestyle will change. Are you ready for that?"

"Are you disappointed?"

"No—surprised."

His reaction betrayed his true feelings; Phil raised her left hand to his lips and affectionately kissed the fingertips.

"Excuse me, dear while I phone Teresa. I'm declaring a holiday to celebrate the happy news."

Teresa detected a tremor in his voice. "Take charge of the office. Margaret and I are spending the rest of the day together.

"Is anything wrong?"

"I'll fill you in, tomorrow. Thanks, Teresa. You're a darling."

Chapter 3

Men's eyes followed Margaret when she left the restaurant with Phil; his gaze focused on her supple walk. With lengthened strides, he closed the distance between them.

With a firm grasp, he guided her to the sidewalk crowded with shoppers, tourists, and workers bound for home. Rather than hail a cab from the predominantly yellow stream of vehicles, hand-in-hand they strolled downtown. On impulse, Phil said, "Let's spend the night in the city."

"Phil—I haven't any change of clothing."

"So what?"

"You know I always prepare in advance."

"No problem."

"Maybe for you . . ."

"We'll pick up whatever we need. It'll be fun."

"You're crazy."

At the first men's clothing store, Phil walked to the shirts. Without hesitation, he made a selection and paid with his charge card. "See how easy . . .?"

"Phil—I can't . . . ."

"That's all the fresh clothing I'll need in the morning."

"I can't live in the same dress."

"Your turn next."

At a lingerie shop with an exotic window display, Phil handed Margaret the charge card. Margaret ignored the erotic articles; garter belts, bikini and split-crotch panties, lacy transparent lingerie. At the nightgowns she held a champagne peignoir, low cut, lace trimmed and, with flowing lines. Smiling, Phil said, "Throw it on the floor—see how it looks—then buy it."

"I can't do that!"

"That's where it will be a minute after I see you wearing it."

18

She playfully slapped his left cheek, hoping the sales clerk did not overhear. Parcels in hand, they strolled down 7th Avenue toward a discount drug store. They bought toothbrushes, a travel tube of toothpaste and sample bottle of Scope™— sufficient for the unplanned overnight stay. The spontaneity of a night at a hotel with a beautiful woman stimulated Phil. *I feel like I'm cheating—and with my own wife!* On the West side of Times Square, they passed the Pussycat Theater™ with its garish lighting and suggestive posters filled with promise of erotic delights. In the box-office, a bored elderly woman, perhaps a grandmother, sold tickets to furtive males, young and old, anxious to enter the theater's dark anonymity.

Phil's anticipation heightened as they neared the Marriott Marquis™. At street level, the vastness of the hotel eluded them—until they looked upward at the towering structure and collided with similarly occupied pedestrians. Once a victim, Phil checked for the safety of his wallet. They entered through revolving doors into the bustling lobby and carrying their plastic bags approached the registration desk. The clerk asked, "Do you have a reservation?"

Phil replied, "Of course . . . . Mr. and Mrs. Phillip Noble."

"I'm sorry; you are not listed."

"My secretary made the reservation."

"We may have a cancellation . . . a suite on the twenty-third floor overlooking Times Square."

"Sounds great."

"How long will you stay?"

"We leave for Chicago in the morning."

The clerk processed Phil's magical charge card. "The Bell Captain will tend to your bags."

"The airline lost our luggage."

Phil signed the register. Margaret's face flushed when the clerk gave their key to the bellhop and said, "Their luggage will be along later." The bellhop nodded knowingly and led them to a battery of elevators. A solid bronze door opened—they had the sensation of stepping into air since the elevator walls were clear glass from floor to ceiling. The lighting exaggerated the speed of ascent as the elevator climbed inside the tower to a dizzy height overlooking the atrium. Margaret held Phil's arm. "How beautiful! I could spend a week here."

The bellhop escorted them to their room, and after a brief explanation of the air conditioning and television controls left with a generous tip. Alone at last, they savored the magic of the evening.

Too early for dinner, sans luggage, the usual shows on television, the hotel directory to read, the king-sized bed invited occupancy. They exchanged meaningful glances. Margaret checked the bathroom. "How luxurious—I'll spend the evening in here." The glistening rose-hued marble walls and a mirrored wall reflected a tub inset in matching marble and large enough for double occupancy. The gold-plated faucets and accessories sparkled. A convenient shelf held complimentary soaps, shampoos, bath powders, and body oils. Stacks of monogrammed towels covered a higher shelf. Margaret poured bubble bath in the rushing water and leisurely disrobed. Above the sound of the water, she said, "I need a warm soothing bath." Carefully she hung her clothing for future use. Pleased with the water's temperature, she slid under the luxurious suds. "Care to join me?" she called. At her invitation, Phil stopped emptying his pockets, dropped his trousers and stepped out of his briefs.

Margaret with only her head visible raised a hand above the foam and beckoned. Phil saw his nude reflection approach her. *Not a pretty sight. How can she find my hairy body attractive? When I look at her, I see perfection.* Conscious of his exposure, he lowered himself into the water—relieved to hide his nakedness.

On impulse, he raised her left foot out of the water and manipulated the sole and toes with his thumbs. He once read that shiatsu, pressure on certain areas of the feet, help relaxation. Margaret smiled. His fingers traveled up her leg gently massaging her calf and continued to mid-thigh. With eyes closed, Margaret leaned back. "You're so talented." Urged on by her praise, Phil lowered her leg into the warm water and repeated the process on the other foot. He kneeled at her side and placed his arm on her shoulders, tipping her slightly forward until her breasts swayed while he massaged her arched neck and loosened her taut shoulders. The sensation in his fingertips traveled through his body.

Phil stepped from the tub, dried his torso. While brushing his teeth, he saw the stubble on his chin reflected in the mirror. Luckily, the medicine cabinet held a disposable razor, shaving gel and after-shave lotion. Clean-shaven and refreshed, Phil draped a dry towel around his waist, pulled back the bedspread, and propped by pillows, waited.

Meanwhile, Margaret dawdled, relaxed by the warm bath and massage. She emerged from the suds like a butterfly leaving the cocoon—slow and deliberate. She dried and powdered her body and slipped into her peignoir. Lack of cosmetics hindered her normal routine of facial masks, cleansers, and night creams. Adapting to the natural look, she arranged her hair to hang loosely. She entered the bedroom like a princess, wearing the peignoir. Facing Phil she asked, "Do you like it?"

"I love it and I love you." He rose from the bed, embraced her while his kisses traveled from her shoulder and neck to her lips. His towel dropped, he held her close, his arousal against her. The gown had several ribbon bows tied at strategic locations that his eager fingers found. Fulfilling his prediction at the lingerie shop, the peignoir joined the towel on the floor. Pressed against each other; their hands explored, desire mounted. Phil led her to the bed. She sat facing him, her hand slowly releasing him as he knelt, his lips teasing her breasts.

As he thought about sharing her with the baby, Phil's libido ebbed. He pictured millions of thrashing spermatozoa futilely banging their heads against the impervious wall of a fertilized ovum. Lacking experience, the mysteries of first pregnancy frightened him. Before knowledge of her pregnancy, Phil would have been ecstatic—now he experienced a strange detachment, like an actor playing a role. The utilitarian thought of these lovely creations, their sole purpose to provide sustenance dampened his ardor. Erotic possibilities fled; his lovemaking became a clinical exercise as biological drawings of the female anatomy depicting the fetus at different stages of development filled his brain. He hesitated before penetrating her and resuming his passionate pretense. He covered her abdomen with kisses—*was the baby aware?* He moved to her inner thighs, gently nipping. Margaret writhed. "Now!" She gasped. He knelt before her offering; . . . failed to enter. Margaret patiently watched him resort to manual dexterity. With gentle, slow mechanical thrusts, he pictured the baby protesting. Margaret responded; she pressed against him—he backed away. He moved like a robot, unable to climax. Certain that she reached orgasm, he faked ejaculation . . . stiffened his body with every muscle taut. He groaned, "I love you!" Phil treated Margaret with gentleness and consideration. She glowed, basking in the attention, and the security of his love. Phil's romantic interlude with Margaret ended in personal disaster; sex with Margaret would never be the same.

After a respectable pause, Phil turned to Margaret; "I'm hungry.

"Then order from room service."

"We could try the The View™."

"I'm tired."

"The food is usually better."

"You go."

"Not without you. This is our night together."

"Look at my hair. I need to repair the wreck you made of me."

"Forget it."

"We'll go later then."

At ten, they rode the glass-walled elevator to The View™, a rotating restaurant offering a changing view of the lights of Manhattan. Phil, famished and piqued at Margaret's earlier refusal, ordered a double martini before dinner; Margaret abstained from her usual Chardonnay® and selected a non-alcoholic fruit drink. Phil raised his glass. "Here's to our family. May we enjoy health, happiness and prosperity." Margaret added, "And love."

*   *   *

Startled by the brilliant morning sun engulfing the room, Phil threw off the covers. Late for work, he showered while Margaret lazily opened her eyes and stretched.

"What if you are late? You're the boss. Come back to bed."

"You're right!"

He returned from the shower and slid in beside her. She screamed, "Are you crazy? You're cold and wet!" She bounded from the bed—Phil caught her and carried her, protesting, into the shower.

Wide-awake after Phil's crazy antics, Margaret packed her new peignoir and his old shirt in plastic bags.

Phil phoned the hotel desk. "Please prepare my bill. Have a limo at the main entrance."

To Margaret he said," Are you packed?"

She held the plastic bags high and smiled. "You're so thoughtful. That's why I love you."

At Veidell, the chauffeur opened the door. Phil lightly kissed Margaret. "I hate to leave you. I'll catch an earlier train. Love you." As he watched the limo merge in traffic, he remembered Margaret's shopping bags. *Damn! Now I'll have to lug them on a crowded train. My evening ended in failure—yet I've never seen Margaret happier—a tribute to my acting abilities. Then why am I depressed? She loves me. I love her—yet, it's different. Is this being a father? Why can't I share Margaret's joy?*

Margaret phoned Phil at noon. "Thanks for the fabulous night. I have the world's most loving husband."

"We did have fun, didn't we?"

"I love you."

"We'll have to do that again."

"Don't forget the Bergdof Goodman™ bags."

Usually, Phil carried his briefcase on the train and read work-related publications. This evening he struggled with Margaret's shopping bags, hoping he would not accidentally leave them on the train. He thought about the baby. *Will it be a boy or girl? What traits will it have—Margaret or mine—perhaps a little of both?*

Chapter 4

During Phil's call from Le Coquilles, Teresa detected strangeness in Phil's voice; she resented the camaraderie that Margaret and Phil shared. Her disappointment carried over into the morning while during her usual office inspection, she imagined celebrating with Phil—anything. When he appeared with a cordial greeting for everyone, her curiosity peaked. *Why was he so cheerful?*

Phil paused at her desk and greeted her with a pleasant, "Good morning, Teresa."

"Good morning, Mister Noble. We missed you yesterday afternoon." Teresa blurted, "What did you celebrate? You promised to tell me."

"Yes, I did. We had a memorable luncheon at Le Coquilles. As we offered a toast, Margaret casually announced her pregnancy. I'm going to be a father! Can you believe it after all these years?" The reality of Phil's disclosure and its implications struck her. She gasped and struggled for control. "Congratulations, Mister Noble. I'm very happy for you." The words soured on her tongue.

"Thanks. I'm hoping for a boy."

Their years of working together brought them close; she knew Phil's moods, preferences in food and clothing, sports and literature . . . his secret sexual desire for her that she colored in her vivid imagination. This was contrary to Teresa's usual approach to a relationship; she enjoyed her lovers based on mutual physical attraction with slight knowledge of their personalities and backgrounds. Her feelings toward Phil were different, increasing with time. *I truly love him!*

Margaret's pregnancy created a challenge, an obstacle to her life with Phil, difficult to overcome but not impossible. Teresa planned for her devious intent to succeed. *There's no use dwelling on the pregnancy. There's nothing I can do about it. Damn Frank for his refusal to divorce me because he's Catholic. The last time he entered a church was our wedding day. Somehow, I must free myself to marry Phil. Margaret complicated the situation.*

The entire day Teresa's demeanor, whenever Phil was near, remained formal and business—like. Her usual fantasies failed to ease her through; she occupied her mind with the drudgery of work. Quitting time arrived slowly.

*   *   *

She reached her apartment, greeted her mother and aunt, hung her coat and purse and sulked in her room until dinner. At the table she said, "I'm not hungry." Sensing trouble, her mother asked, "What's bothering you? It's not that time, is it?"

"No—my life is at a dead end. I have no future. I work and return at night to this cramped apartment. That's not enough! I'm lonely—need a man in my life—someone to love me."

Unaware of Teresa's fascination with Phil, her mother encouraged her. "You're a beautiful girl. You should not have problems. Any man would be crazy for you."

In broken English Teresa's aunt added, "Old Haitian woman. Mambo. Helps people." Eagerly, Teresa asked, "What's her phone number?"

"No phone. She knows. Building six, 6D."

That's on the sixth floor! 666, numbers associated with the devil—is it coincidence?

Anxious to meet this unusual woman, Teresa finished dinner with a glass of red wine for courage. It was an hour before darkness; building six cast a long shadow. She entered and through habit bypassed the elevator. Short of breath, she approached the graffiti covered door marked 6D and raised her hand to knock. A crackling voice said, "Come in."

In a different world, dark except for the dim illumination of a dozen candles haphazardly placed, she saw shelves with jars and metal containers filled with strange substances. Burning wax and incense intensified the aura of mystery. A wide-backed rocking chair which appeared to move of its own volition, faced away from her.

"Do not fear. Come, dear."

Teresa approached the woman. Gold caps on her teeth flashed in the candlelight when she smiled. Brown leather sandals showed below the hem of her voluminous red skirt. Strings of beads and chains around her neck covered the front of her long-sleeved flowered blouse. Beaded and metal bracelets adorned her wrists and jangled as she motioned Teresa to sit.

Nervous, Teresa settled her body on the needlepoint cushion of a dark mahogany chair with an ornately carved high backrest and legs carved in the shape of a claw holding a glass ball. Teresa's fingers naturally fell into four carved grooves of the armrests. Within the chair's embrace she stared, fascinated by the mambo's dark wrinkled face.

"Call me Mama Louise."

"I need help."

"What is your problem?"

"I love a man—he's married."

"And you want him?"

"My husband won't divorce me because he's Catholic. We've been separated for five years."

"You are both married? Serious problems."

"I need that divorce to marry my true love."

"Spells are dangerous and sometimes do not work as expected. Careful what you ask."

"What do you expect of me in return for your help?"

"I live simply. To keep my jars and containers stocked and candles, I get fifty dollars for a love potion and one hundred dollars for a spell." Both can be serious. Again, what is your problem?"

"I haven't lived with my husband, Frank, for five years, yet he refuses to divorce me so I can move on with my life."

"What would you like me to do?"

"Change his mind—cast a spell or whatever it is you do."

"Are you sure? I need a piece of his hair or fingernail clippings—some part of him—a piece of clothing or jewelry. With these and the money you will have your wish."

Teresa agreed and left the weirdness of Mama Louise's apartment for the real world. *How can I get close to Frank after I threw him out of my home? Many times, I told him I hated him. I thought Mama Louise would influence Frank to agree to the divorce without my involvement I'll sleep on it. Tomorrow I might view the situation in a new light.*

Tomorrow came and went, as did a number of tomorrows—a week passed. Teresa had no idea how to get the items Mama Louise required. Every waking thought dwelled on her problem.

Teresa awakened in the throes of a nightmare. Frank was raping her as she struggled to escape. *Why didn't I think of it earlier? Rape Frank! I'll get all the ingredients I need by attacking him. Only he won't know it; he'll think I reconsidered and want to return to him.* Her scheme evolved at a feverish pitch. She anxiously waited for dawn and the start her offensive.

*   *   *

Next morning, Phil found her in a cheerful mood. "You seemed preoccupied all week. Glad you're back."

Teresa smiled. ". . . a little personal matter to resolve."

Later, Teresa searched for Frank's work number in the Rolodex™. It was important that she talk to him before noon—before he left with his shipping—platform buddies for a liquid lunch. Teresa didn't want him to start drinking and forget her message. Dialing the number, she mentally rehearsed her sales pitch. A gruff voice amid the sounds of forklifts and delivery trucks, answered unintelligibly. Certain she had the correct number, Teresa said, "Please, may I speak to Frank?"

The voice forced Teresa to distance the receiver from her ear. "Hey, Frank. Get your ass over here. Some broad on the line—asking for you." Frank snatched the phone, "Yeah?"

"It's Teresa." Frank smiled, perplexed after their last encounter.

"I'm sorry—how I treated you last week. I was shocked to find you in my apartment. Can we talk?"

"Oh—it's OK. I guess we both said mean things."

"Meet me after work for a drink at the Silver Palms™. I can be there by six . . . ."

During their courtship, Frank and Teresa frequented the Silver Palms™, a tavern two blocks from his apartment south of Queens Boulevard in Sunnyside. *Strange that she wants to meet there—unless she reconsidered.* "You guys go without me. I have a date tonight—with my wife."

"Frank. Are you there? Answer me—please."

"I'm here, Teres'—it will be my pleasure. I'll be the guy with the red beard."

"Don't be sarcastic. I'm trying to make amends. Of course I'll recognize you."

"Sorry. I promise I'll behave. See you tonight then—at six."

I did it! He believed me.

After work, Teresa entered the women's lounge to prepare for her date. She changed her subdued pink lipstick for a hot red and applied eye shadow. She wanted Frank to respond—as if that were necessary with his nearly celibate life without her. With a seductive smile at the mirror, pleased by her reflection, she moistened her lips. *That should do the trick.* She laughed, savoring the promise of freedom from Frank.

Leaving Veidell, she hailed a taxi for the ride over the 59th Street Bridge to Long Island City and Sunnyside. Fortunately, the driver understood English and knew the way. The horrendous rush hour traffic backed up for blocks at the approaches to the bridge. She envied the people who lived on Roosevelt Island and commuted by tram, swaying over the East River in a cabin suspended by cables. Engrossed by the people boarding for their aerial journey, she relaxed. Once on the bridge, the traffic moved and within ten minutes, she arrived at the Silver Palms™. In good spirits, Teresa paid the driver the metered amount plus a generous tip. She hesitated—the romantic luster she associated with the tavern had tarnished—the silver palm trees painted on the inside of the front windows had dulled and started to peel. The inside was unchanged—potted artificial silver palm trees with silver coconuts strategically placed provided privacy at selected tables.

Office and blue-collar workers, stragglers from the happy hour, lined the bar. Teresa searched for Frank; she was early and he had not arrived.

Straight from work, Frank went to his apartment to remove any trace of female companionship and to shower the grime of the shipping platform. He accomplished all while watching the clock—*can't keep Teresa waiting.*

Meanwhile, Teresa fidgeted in a corner booth in view of the door. At six, an anxious Frank entered looking for her. *Another six. How appropriate. That fits in with the sixth floor and apartment 6D. It is an omen; I will succeed.*

He smiled when he saw her. Fearing another disappointment, uncertain of his welcome, he approached. He leaned down and kissed her offered left cheek. Her scent intensified his desire. *Was this happening?*

"Am I happy to see you! At our last meeting, I thought we were finished. Weren't we obnoxious? I'm truly sorry."

"Me too. Forget our hideous behavior—call a truce and enjoy this evening—wherever it may lead."

"I agree."

"You order for me."

Although a confirmed beer drinker, Frank summoned the waiter and ordered two Manhattans. He loved the way Teresa raised the maraschino cherry from her glass, held it by the stem and teased it with her lips before she allowed it to enter her mouth. He gave her the cherry from his Manhattan. Frank limited himself to one drink to keep a clear head for an evening of promise.

Their date appeared enjoyable—Frank well mannered and Teresa spellbound by his attention. He reached across the table for her hand, held it near his beard and then kissed her fingertips. Teresa felt the hair on the nape of her neck bristle, but said nothing. She forced herself to bear with Frank. Her tiny hand, held captive by his massive fingers, at last slipped free.

Frank asked, "Are you hungry? I am."

"Not really."

"We could go to one of our quaint neighborhood ethnic restaurants for Greek, Italian, Chinese, White Castle™—you name it—or my place and I'll whip up one of my customary frozen gourmet feasts."

She hoped for this opening. "That sounds interesting. I'd love to . . . . It's rather crowded here."

He offered his hand. "Then, let's go!" Astounded at his good fortune, Frank placed Teresa's jacket on her shoulders. Although tempted to hurry before she changed her mind, he shortened his strides to match hers and imagined a night with Teresa.

Solicitously, he opened the door to the vestibule and held her arm. Aware of how her legs tapered from her trim body, Frank trailed her up the single flight of stairs. With trembling hand, he found the key. She entered, dreading her distasteful task.

Frank activated a dimmer switch for the lamp near the sofa. From a hidden source, soft romantic music sounded. In the kitchenette, he shattered the seductive setting with the bright bluish glare of a circular neon light. At the open freezer door Frank asked, "Would you like Beef Stroganoff® or Chicken Cordon Bleu®?"

Teresa, anxious to complete her mission said, "Never mind the food! Turn off the light." Frank threw the dinners into the freezer, turned off the glaring light, wiped his cold moist hands on his pants and hurried to the sofa. Involuntarily, she moved away. "Where's your bathroom?" Frank pointed down the long hallway. His pulse quickened at the sound of water through the thin wood-paneled door. *She's preparing herself for me!*

Teresa checked her purse for the items required. She removed two condoms from their protective envelops and placed them in an open plastic bag for quick access. She renewed her lipstick and sprayed Frank's cologne on her neck. She returned smiling. "Did you miss me?"

". . . sure did."

"Your beard is straggly and unkempt. Don't you ever trim it?"

"Why?"

"I can't see your lips through all that underbrush."

She returned to the bathroom and found scissors in the medicine cabinet. "Come here and I'll style that scruffy beard."

She placed a towel around his neck. The scissors clicked near Frank's ear and worked along his bushy red beard. Teresa slipped strands of hair into a plastic bag and then held a mirror to his face, "Don't you look better?" Without a glance, he agreed.

She left while Frank brushed loose hairs from his neck and shoulders. To get all the hairs off, he removed his shirt. He filled the washbasin and scrubbed his chest, neck and underarms. After attending to personal hygiene, encouraged by Teresa's behavior, he joined her on the sofa.

She involuntarily admired his bronzed well-developed arms—chest hairy enough to be a continuation of his beard. He stood in silence before her. She rose from the sofa and played her fingers upon his chest. With lowered head, her lips teased nipples barely visible through the hairy mat. He shuddered. Encouraged, he ventured to open her blouse. She shoved his hands away. Her response puzzled him.

To speed the process, she had removed her bra in the bathroom. Now, she slowly opened her blouse and dropped it on the floor. Her pointed breasts, invited his grasp. With more of a hiss than a whisper she said, "Relax and let me take care of you." It was so long since Frank had a woman that relaxation was physically impossible. She firmly held his hands and guided him down to the floor. He lay fascinated, as she removed her slacks and stood over him. He reached upward; she avoided his grasp, moved toward his feet and stood facing him.

"Relax. I'll take care of everything. Trust me." She knelt and removed his loafers. With deft fingers, she opened his belt and zipper and pulled his trousers and briefs off in one swift motion. She avoided his hands, removed her bikini panties and slipped protection on Frank.

"What are you doing? We never used that before."

"We will now. I don't know how many women you've slept with."

Frank thought about his chronic impotence, "I assure you. It's not necessary."

"Well, it's this way or the highway—your choice!"

In his state of arousal, Frank willingly agreed to her terms. She stood over him, her feet planted on either side of his hips; her femininity tantalized him.

"Keep your hands down or I'll leave."

Slowly she lowered her body guiding him to a slight penetration and then to torture him abruptly pulled away. In a deliberate and slow movement, she went for full penetration and felt the pulse of his ejaculate as he thrust upward. As his body stiffened, she backed off and reached into his trouser pocket for a handkerchief. Removing the condom, she wiped him clean and placed the handkerchief in the plastic bag. *A personal item stained with his semen will make an extraordinary spell.*

To her surprise, she experienced a fierce pleasure in dominating him that opened a new flood of sexuality. Before he fully recovered, Teresa coaxed another erection. With the second condom in place, she intended rape with a vengeance. While keeping his hands from touching, she ground her pelvis with her entire weight. Frank pleaded, "Enough! Stop! I can't take anymore." Secretly enjoying her sadistic attack, she persisted. The louder his complaints, the rougher she treated him. "You wouldn't want me to leave? Would you?" She ignored his protests until he didn't move.

Teresa anxious to remove any trace of Frank, showered, dressed and checked the security of her purse's contents before leaving. Her absence would increase his torment. Frank lay motionless on the floor. She wasn't sure if he was breathing—and she didn't care!

She walked with an odd gait to the Silver Palms™. There she called a cab from the business cards posted by the phone. She winced when the cab hit a deep pothole and imagined tomorrow's newspaper headline, 'Man Dead from Sexual Attack.' Her pain was a small price for her freedom. She recalled the motionless Frank, recumbent on the floor. *Is it possible I killed him?*

*   *   *

Frank called out, "Teres', Are you there?" No answer.

Disappointed, he arose shivering from the breeze that blew the curtains inward. He wanted her essence on his skin forever, but practicality won. Despite the noisy plumbing, he turned on the shower faucet. *I'll deal with complaints from the apartment below tomorrow.* The pulsing water brought partial relief. *She was a wild woman! I'll never be able to work. She crippled me.* In bed, he placed a pillow between his knees to relieve the pressure. Restless, he watched for the sun to rise.

At work, Frank puzzled over Teresa's sudden reversal of attitude. *Does she still love me after a five-year separation? Why did she greet me at the Silver Palms™ as if she missed me? Afterward, why . . . go to my apartment? She certainly wasn't hungry. Was she that deprived of sex? No. She could seduce any man. Why her sudden departure? What is she doing now?* Frank mulled over the events of last night. Debilitated, he felt, the suffering was worth it. The vision of Teresa standing over him triggered a painful stirring. *God! Why did I ever leave her?*

*   *   *

On the subway, Teresa guarded the precious contents of her purse that would puzzle any thief. She could not risk leaving the plastic bag in her apartment; her aunt or mother might dispose of it with the trash. Anyway, a repeat performance with Frank was unthinkable.

During lunch hour, impatient in line at the bank, she scanned the customers for shady characters. At the teller's window, Teresa withdrew a hundred dollars from her meager savings account and placed it in her purse alongside her precious ingredients. At the office with Phil in Chicago on business, time passed slowly.

*   *   *

Anxious to deliver her acquisitions to Mama Louise, she arrived at apartment 6D. Nervous, she raised her hand to knock. Mama Louise called, "Come in, daughter." In flickering candlelight, the rocking chair moved. Mama Louise motioned Teresa to sit in the chair with claws for legs. Teresa complied like an obedient child.

"Mama Louise, I have money and the ingredients for the spell. Can you do it tonight?"

"A spell is what you want, darlin'?"

"Yes. I need my freedom."

"Why?"

"My husband won't divorce me."

"What do you want of me?"

"Change his mind."

"That may be difficult."

"Do what you have to do."

"Then I'll proceed."

From jars and containers, Mama Louise gathered powders, plants and other mysterious ingredients and mixed them on a black marble slab. After lighting two candles, she chanted and. threw a pinch on the flame, which flared up with a brilliance that made Teresa shield her eyes. She emptied the contents of the plastic bag along with the mixture into an earthenware urn. After more incantations and gestures, she extinguished one candle and placed the other in front of the urn. "A candle will burn until you get your wish. Then, I'll destroy the urn and its contents."

"Thank you for your help, Mama Louise." She left anticipating freedom from her husband.

*   *   *

A week after Frank recuperated, he phoned Teresa at Veidell; she cut him short. "Frank—I'm busy. I can't talk now." In the evening, he phoned her at home, "Teresa—I thought you might join me tomorrow after work."

"Never! After the way you treated me the last time?"

He unsuccessfully searched his conscience. "If I did anything—anything wrong, I'm sorry. Why are you angry with me?"

Teresa kept him on the defensive. "You know . . . ."

"No—I don't. Please tell me—so I . . . ."

Teresa left the phone off-hook.

He phoned her home daily. Her mother screened all calls. Upon hearing Frank, she responded, ". . . not home!" Frank drowned his frustration in beer and whiskey—ending every evening drunk.

*   *   *

Three weeks later after work, his clothes wet from intermittent rain, Frank stopped at a bar on Jackson Avenue. The aroma of pickles and beer whetted his appetite. He ordered a pastrami sandwich on rye and a stein of draft beer. Beer followed beer, until the football players on the television blurred. Following the well-worn path in the varnished floor, he left the barstool only to make room for more beer. Frank needed sleep. At midnight, he left.

The night air and rain refreshed his face. Distant lightning flashes followed by rolling thunder forewarned an intense storm. An elevated train passing overhead showered the wet cobblestones with sparks from a defective arcing contact shoe; the bright flashes affected Frank's hazy vision. His balance impaired, Frank managed to cross Jackson Avenue. He staggered down Bridge Plaza South and spotted a taxi on the other side. The slippery cobblestones, the steel pillars of the overhead IRT™ elevated trains and traffic from the 59th Street Bridge made the area hazardous; tow-truck drivers parked on side streets ready to respond to inevitable accidents. Frank crossed to a pillar and leaned against it. He saw the cab driver prepare to leave. Frank shouted and stepped from the safety of the pillar. A screech of brakes . . . a dull thud . . . then nothing. At the instant of death, the candle Mama Louise placed in front of the urn flickered—the flame extinguished by a mysterious breeze. Smoke from the smoldering wick drifted upward.

The car swerved wildly on the slick cobblestones before stopping. The driver reached the crumpled body and placed trembling fingers on Frank's neck—no pulse. He checked for a breath—nothing. Blood flowed from Frank's ear and mouth.

The driver returned to his car for flares. A passing police car stopped and turned on flashing warning lights; the officer saw the body on the pavement and radioed for an ambulance. He then approached the driver and asked, "What happened?"

The driver identified himself as off-duty cop from the Mid-Manhattan precinct. "I was on my way home when this guy stepped out from behind a pillar directly in front of me. No way could I avoid hitting him. I think he's dead."

Within minutes, the ambulance arrived and the Emergency Medical Technicians rushed to Frank's side. They found no vital signs.

*   *   *

The next day, a detective checked Frank's wallet. From an ID card, he contacted Frank's employer—personnel records named Teresa, spouse. He wrote Teresa's address in his notebook.

That evening a loud insistent knock on her door startled Teresa. Thinking it was Frank, she shouted, "What do you want?"

"Police!" She opened the door, still held by a chain lock. Seeing the badge, she removed the chain.

"Are you Mrs. Teresa McCormick?"

"Yes?"

"I have bad news. Your husband died in a serious accident. I'm sorry."

"What happened?"

"He was drinking and he stepped in front of a car coming off the bridge."

"Did he suffer?"

"I don't believe so, judging by his blood alcohol level."

Teresa's face paled. *Mama Louise's spell! He's here to arrest me.*

"I need you to identify him". He handed her a note. "This is where his body lies. I'm sorry. Will you be all right?"

"We've been separated for five years, but there's always the precious memory of our years together."

*   *   *

She phoned Phil. "A detective came to inform me that my husband Frank was hit by a car and died. I have to arrange his burial. I'm his only relative."

"I'm sorry. Take all the time you need."

At the morgue, she experienced a chill upon viewing his cold corpse on the slab. A sense of guilt—that she was somehow responsible haunted her. She left the coroner's office with the death certificate.

From a public coin phone, Teresa called Frank's Benefits Office. "This is the wife of Frank McCormick, will you help me make the arrangements for my deceased husband."

"Yes, Mrs. McCormick. The police said you might contact us."

"Can I meet with a representative today?"

"Will three this afternoon, be convenient? Bring the death certificate. It will expedite the process."

Teresa met the Benefits Representative, a Korean girl about ten years younger than her. The girl listed all of Teresa's entitlements; a death benefit of five thousand dollars to cover the burial expenses and a forty-five thousand dollar group life insurance policy to provide for Teresa. Teresa found difficulty portraying the bereaved widow. Struggling to hide her elation, she thanked the girl.

Unable to locate Frank's siblings or relatives she arranged a poorly attended funeral Mass, and then buried him in Calvary Cemetery. Dressed in a demure black dress and black hat, the lone mourner sobbed uncontrollably as they lowered his casket into an unmarked grave.

Was Frank's death truly an accident or had I caused it with Mama Louise's spell? I'll never know!

Chapter 5

With feigned sorrow, Teresa accepted the $50,000 from Mister Palmer. The insurance agent hoping to sell additional policies personally delivered the check. A brief survey of the apartment dimmed his prospects for a sale. The furniture, of flea-market quality, though spotless, was uninsurable; no self-respecting thief would bother . . . . Teresa's mother and aunt eavesdropped from the kitchen. He inquired whether they had insurance—disappointed to find that modest policies covered the costs of no-frills burials. Since Teresa and Frank were childless, the agent's prospects dwindled. Teresa cared less about coverage for her demise; the present concerned her.

Despite his sympathy for her loss, he departed with a handshake and Teresa's gratitude. Then, unable to restrain her joy, she danced while waving the check over her head. In the morning, Teresa deposited $30,000 to her meager savings account. Delighted at the passbook balance, she opened her first checking account with $19,000 and withheld $1,000 cash. *Thanks to Frank.*

With time to settle affairs, she decided to find an apartment. Determined to leave Manhattan, she considered a place on Roosevelt Island . . . commute via the aerial tramway instead of the subway. However, rentals were beyond her newly acquired means. A real estate agent showed her several apartments in Queens; she found fault with each. Finally, in Kew Gardens, she chanced upon a sunny third floor furnished studio apartment. The spacious room and modern furniture contrasted sharply with her present lodgings. Teresa loved the independence and privacy of her new quarters. Her hand trembled as she signed the lease and wrote her first check. For once in her life, she controlled her destiny.

The real estate agent handed her the keys and instructed her on use of the buzzer and intercom system to permit entry to the building. The unaccustomed quiet and the odor of brass polish and other cleaning agents in the lobby, elevator and hallway awed her. She lived in a new world, devoid of the constant sound of children, the graffiti covered walls, the reeking stairwells and elevators. She wouldn't be ashamed to invite Phil inside this apartment. Pleased with herself, she went on a shopping spree.

At an appliance store on Queen's Boulevard, drawn by a sign that promised a charge account with no interest for ninety days, a clerk gave her an application form. Teresa proudly listed her bank. The manager's phone call resulted in immediate approval. With her new charge account, she bought a color television; delivery and set up scheduled for later that day. Money in the bank certainly made things happen.

Teresa returned to her apartment to wait for delivery of the TV. After installation, she left the apartment and traveled to Manhattan in style—by car service limousine. She dreaded breaking the news to her aunt and mother—expecting a battle. But first she had important business with Mama Louise.

Before reaching apartment 6D, she removed a fifty-dollar bill from her purse. *The sight of money might tempt the old mambo to increase her price—although with supernatural powers Mama Louise probably knew the exact amount of my wealth.*

Teresa raised her hand to knock. Mama Louise called out, "Enter, child!" Teresa let herself in.

"I sense happiness." Mama Louise said—it was almost a question.

Teresa lost in the chair that had claws for legs, faced Mama Louise. "You helped me—more than I ever imagined. I need you again. There is a man I love, who loves another. I want him to love me. I know with your powers anything is possible."

"Be careful what you ask; what you get is not always what you want."

"I want him. Is fifty dollars enough?"

Mama Louise smiled with the knowledge that Teresa could well afford more. Nevertheless, from several containers, she placed unrecognizable contents into a clay bowl. She ground the ingredients into a light gray powder while chanting magical words. Then, poured the powder into a leather pouch, which she gave Teresa.

"Use only a pinch in his coffee or tea. It will make him desire you. If the wrong person drinks it, I can't help you."

Teresa eagerly grabbed the pouch—in her hand, she held power over Phil's love. She paid Mama Louise and left with confidence after her previous success.

*   *   *

Teresa kept secret Frank's insurance money and her good fortune. Her mother questioned her lateness. "I had things to do. I'm moving out! I've leased an apartment in Queens."

Teresa's mother was overjoyed until she realized the move did not include her. People in the next apartment heard her bemoan abandonment by her ungrateful daughter. Teresa, accustomed to such outbreaks, started packing. She hurriedly stuffed clothing, costume jewelry, cosmetics and her camera with miscellaneous items in two old suitcases. In an attempt to quell her mother's tears and anger, she caused a greater uproar. With her luggage, she made her getaway—took the elevator to the lobby and hailed the first available taxi.

As the cab bumped across the 59th Street Bridge, she recalled her date with Frank—how he lost his life—how this bridge became a symbol of her freedom and independence. Joy for her future overcame fleeting guilt.

It was dark when she arrived in Kew Gardens. The subdued lighting along the walkway and sparkling chandelier in the foyer welcomed her. After she paid the driver and added a generous tip, he carried her luggage to the front entrance. The firm click of her key in the lock, gave her an unusual sense of security. He carried the luggage into the lobby, then left. The well-lighted elevator appeared secure and dependable. *This is the way to live!*

Alone in her room, she turned on the television. The ten o'clock news broke the unaccustomed silence; tired of the reported violence, she turned it off. She bathed, changed into her nightgown and slipped between cool spotless sheets. Recalling the events since she became rich, she fell asleep—the leather pouch beside her pillow.

*   *   *

Teresa returned to Veidell's the next day. After consoling Teresa on her loss, he sent her on a personal errand. *Phil has nerve, asking me to buy gifts for his wife!* With reluctance, she wound her way through the crowd of Christmas shoppers carrying colorful bags and presents. She skirted the layers of children and adults watching animated figures in department store windows. She walked around the line of people waiting for admission to the Radio City Music Hall Christmas extravaganza and avoided the seedy bell-ringing Santas on every corner, guarding their red chimneys or kettles.

At the Saks Fifth Avenue™ cosmetics counter, she bought Margaret's favorite perfume, Obsession™. Because of Margaret's pregnancy, suits or dresses were impractical. She settled on a long white furry housecoat, rather than sexy lingerie and hoped Margaret would look like an over-sized *Bichon Frise*. With the rest of Phil's money, she purchased a 14k gold pendant on a chain in the shape of "#1Mom". Her distasteful task completed, she returned to the office. The pleasure Phil expressed with her choices annoyed her. Apparently, the minuscule amount of Mama Louise's love potion that Teresa placed in Phil's morning coffee failed.

Chapter 6

It was the time of corporate Christmas parties; before budgetary constraints, legal responsibilities and moral considerations became an issue. Teresa anticipated Veidell's party as an opportunity to get close to Phil. The company's annual Christmas party was always a high point in Teresa's life. She enjoyed the preparation and planning. Besides, active participation provided a welcome break in daily routine. With Alicia's help, she decorated the office and arranged with the caterer to insure an abundance of alcoholic drinks. The parties at Veidell were notorious for their wantonness; several marriages disintegrated afterwards. Liquor loosened tongues—to curious management this party was the perfect conduit of information. After a few drinks, everyone became pals. Mistletoe hung everywhere giving the lecherous a distinct license.

By afternoon preparations were complete. Along one side of the office at a long buffet table, three white-gloved servers dispensed the hot dishes. Flanking them on either side were tables with salads, cheeses from many countries and out-of-season fruit. In the opposite corner, two bartenders served liquor. The disc jockey played Christmas carols at a subdued level from over-powered speakers to encourage conversation. At first the party started with a respectful murmur of happy voices, increasing in volume in proportion to the food and liquor consumed. The music became louder and couples, that had barely said "Hi" to each other, paired under the ubiquitous mistletoe. Others danced, in newfound intimacy.

Teresa mingled with her senses tuned for Phil's presence. Homing in, she grasped his arm and separated him from a group of associates. "Phil! These people don't want to talk shop! Come on. Let's dance." Once on the floor, she stumbled on the pretext of unaccustomed liquor. When the music stopped, she glanced upward at the mistletoe, placed her arms around Phil's neck and planted a soulful kiss on his lips. Her body molded into his while the kiss lingered. Then with lips nearly touching, she whispered, "Merry Christmas, boss." His face, red with embarrassment, registered surprise and shock. They danced to the sounds of "White Christmas®." She held him close—their bodies meshed—her cheek on his shoulder. With upturned face, she brushed her lips on his white collar, branding it with the red lipstick. *Let Margaret wonder who put it there!* She clung to him like ivy, and felt his wordless reaction. Phil, uncomfortable, excused himself with need of the Men's room. Instead, he went into his office and phoned Margaret.

"I'll be on the 7:39 train. Can you meet me at the station?"

"Certainly. How's the party?"

"Great. I wish you were here. See you soon."

". . . love you."

Meanwhile, Teresa downed a double scotch at the bar. When Phil returned, he found her not a little tipsy but drunk. In her state, she could never get safely home. He felt a responsibility for her.

"Teresa, how much did you drink?"

"I'm not drunk!"

"I think it's time to leave."

"I'm fine."

"You're going home!"

Phil got her purse and held her coat. After several futile attempts to put her arms in the sleeves, he placed it over her shoulders and fastened the top button. He helped her down the elevator, through the lobby, to the sidewalk and then hailed a taxi. He intended to give the driver her address and pay the fare. While Phil assisted Teresa into the taxi, she lost consciousness and crumpled to the floor. Halfway in the cab, he lifted her to the seat. Torn between catching the 7:39 train with Margaret waiting at the station and Teresa's helplessness, Phil had no choice.

Teresa, awakened by the sound of tires on the steel grating of the 59th Street Bridge, discovered Phil holding her. She nestled her head on his shoulder comforted by his warmth. Reluctant to speak, she moved her body closer. He looked down at her, "Are you all right?"

"What happened? Where are we?"

"You were in no condition to get home alone."

"That last drink was my downfall. I'm sorry. You think I'm a terrible lush, don't you? How can I thank you for helping me?"

"Sleep and I'll wake you when we get there."

She snuggled closer, warm, content, and oblivious to the world. Phil saw no escape from the predicament. *What could I do? She's so fragile and helpless.*

The taxi stopped at the entrance to Teresa's apartment complex. She wakened when Phil asked the driver, "What's the fare?" She stretched slowly, like a cat and opened her sleepy eyes. She clung to him, averse to surrender the warmth of his body and enter the cold night air. He pried her hands from his arm so he could reach the door latch. After paying, he lifted Teresa from the cab and half-carried her to the door, where he searched in her purse for the key. His arms ached from Teresa's weight while she clung to him for support. Inside the foyer, the wait for the elevator seemed endless. *Margaret is waiting in the dark at the train station.* Fortunately, Teresa did not have many keys on her key ring.

Teresa had slept off most of her stupor, and having maneuvered Phil into her apartment, took advantage of the opportunity.

"How can I thank you? Coffee? I have instant."

"No—I haven't time. Margaret's at the station."

". . . a few minutes while I shower. My head is woozy. I'd feel safer."

"Well . . . hurry. Margaret is waiting. I'm already late."

Since Margaret announced her pregnancy, Phil had a problem making love; he thought of her as a mother figure and avoided intimacy. When Teresa left the bathroom door slightly ajar, Phil heard the interrupted flow of the water upon her skin and envisioned her washing her body. He waited while she dried her body, her arms, breasts, thighs. The fragrance of bath powder reached him. Fighting his impulse, he stood up prepared to leave and called out, "Teresa, I'm leaving."

Suddenly, she appeared before him, wrapped in a bath towel with a green holly leaf and red berry print in Christmas motif. Her damp hair hung in tight curls. Without makeup, she had the appealing freshness of a child. Astounded, Phil blurted, "You look like a Christmas present!"

"I am . . . for you." She extended her arms toward him; the towel dropped. She was more beautiful than he had imagined. He was stunned—unable to move. She reached out with and slowly pulled his face downward. He trembled—his lips touched her breast—he inhaled her fragrance. His knees weakened along with his willpower as he allowed her to remove his jacket and tie. His trembling hands assisted with his remaining clothes. The subdued light softened every curve. In close embrace, she fondled him with roving fingers and gently led him to the bed. She lowered herself, spreading her offering before him—pink flesh—rose petals moist with drops of morning dew and traces of love potion.

"I'm sorry." he apologized. "It's been so long. Did I disappoint you?"

"Hold still; enjoy our closeness." As he recaptured his virility, Teresa matched his movements, slowly increasing the tempo. Animal sounds escaped their lips. Phil, exhausted remained in position. *Why didn't I experience that sensation with Margaret—the times we make love? MARGARET! She's waiting at the train station!* Uncoupling, he gathered his clothing, ran into the bathroom and thoroughly washed. He feared Margaret might detect his infidelity. He tried to remove the lipstick on his collar, and then decided to give Margaret a casual explanation. "After all, it was a Christmas party. How should I know who put it there?" When he returned to the bedroom, Teresa urged, "Please—don't go." She kissed him on the neck, branding him with a hickey.

Hearing the elevator door close, she slid into bed, savoring the truth of Phil's seed within her. She reached for a calendar marked with the date of her last period and calculated her fertile time. Disappointed, she threw the calendar at the wall. Like Margaret, she wanted to carry Phil's child.

Pleased with her progress, Teresa recounted the day's events. *By giving Phil complete control over me, I controlled him. My helplessness brought Phil to me. I never drank to inebriation until now. Instinct prompted me to down the double scotch. My total dependence brought Phil to my apartment, without discernible aggression on my part. I'll continue the helpless, dependent, childlike role—feed Phil's ego and present a direct opposite of Margaret's independent personality. Then Phil could nurture and protect me.*

Phil, panic-stricken by guilt, attempted to hail a taxi on Queens Boulevard. Stores were closing and taxis were scarce. Luckily, one stopped across the thoroughfare to discharge passengers. Phil whistled and yelled waving his arms like a maniac. Desperate, risking his life, he wove through the fast-moving traffic. "Jamaica train station. Hurry!"

*   *   *

Furious, Margaret waited in her car, occasionally starting the engine for heat, and then turning it off in fear of carbon monoxide poisoning. Alone and vulnerable, except for her dog, she anxiously watched the trains arrive.

"Brandy, I guess he's not on that train either,"

She was tempted to leave and let Phil take a taxi home, but she shivered from the cold and a sense of dread. *Did he have an accident? Did he drink too much? Was he mugged and lying in an alley? Was he helpless in some dark recess of Penn Station?* She turned to restless Brandy for comfort.

"Patience, old girl."

Brandy tail wagged furiously; she recognized Phil's shadowy figure approaching from the darkness.

Relieved, Margaret sighed—*he's all right.* Phil entered the passenger side door and petted Brandy.

"You wouldn't believe what a terrible night I had."

"You could have phoned?"

"I tried but you already left."

He leaned over Brandy and kissed Margaret's right cheek. Although she detected a faint odor of alcohol, he appeared sober.

"What happened? I was worried when you didn't arrive on the 7:39 . . . ."

Phil decided to tell the truth, omitting anything harmful. "I had an emergency. Teresa got drunk."

"That's an emergency?"

"She passed out as I put her in a cab. I couldn't leave her. I felt responsible for her safety. At her apartment, I walked her to the door. She tried to kiss me on the cheek in appreciation but I avoided her. She invited me in for coffee, which I declined. I wished her a Merry Christmas and left. When I reached the street, the taxi had gone; I neglected to tell him to wait. I walked to Queens Boulevard. It's difficult to get a taxi before Christmas. As I walked toward the subway, I caught a taxi that stopped to discharge passengers. Finally, at Jamaica Station, I boarded the first train to Merrick. I thought I would never get here; the train stopped at every station. I pictured you waiting. Thank God I'm home." He was so convincing, he almost believed himself.

"I'm happy that you're here and safe. Horrible images ran through my mind, when you weren't on the 7:39 or the following trains. Brandy worried too." Brandy climbed on him. Phil pushed her snout away as she detected the unfamiliar scent of Teresa. *Thank God, dogs can't talk.* "Brandy! Stop!"

Phil showered with a liberal amount of floral scented bath gel, and then shaved, dousing his face with after-shave lotion. Margaret interpreted his actions as preparation for love. *Weeks passed since sexual intercourse; perhaps he needed the liquor.* She took extra care and wore her champagne peignoir that ended up on the floor that unforgettable night at the Marriott™. As she slid into bed, beside him, Phil reached over to extinguish the lamp on the night table. The collar of his pajama top moved downward and revealed Teresa's hickey. *Lies! All lies!* Margaret did not confront him. She shivered, covered herself and turned her back toward him.

Chapter 7

New Year's Eve, Mister Veidell declared a half-day holiday to observe the arrival of 1975. Phil left his private office to wish his subordinates a happy and prosperous New Year with a sincere handshake for everyone including Teresa. She smiled secretively at his contrived indifference. Both intended to continue their relationship.

That evening Phil and Margaret watched as the television cameras swept over the celebrating crowd at Times Square. The ball covered with hundreds of white lights slid down the greased pole with an urgency to signal the New Year. Bedlam ensued in the streets when the ball reached bottom and the numerals 1975 pulsated in brilliant lights. They exchanged wishes for a Happy New Year with a glass of champagne and a kiss—both flat. Margaret said, "I've had a long day and I'm tired. I'm going to bed." As she left, her polite and distant demeanor irritated him.

New Year's Day, Margaret slept late, skipped breakfast and lazed the morning away. Phil attributed her unusual behavior to pregnancy. *Our life isn't the same since the Christmas party. How much did Margaret know or suspect?*

That evening Phil announced, "The office is moving to another building and I may work late at times. I didn't buy a monthly train ticket because I intend to drive. You won't have to wait at the station on these bitter-cold nights. I don't want you to catch a cold while carrying our child." With this pronouncement, he arranged for time to resume his affair.

*   *   *

The morning traffic was heavier than Phil expected. Instead of relaxing, reading a trade journal or dozing on the train, he had to be constantly alert, making decisions and maneuvering while distracted by thoughts of Teresa.

In the afternoon, Phil phoned Margaret.

"I have to work tonight. Don't hold dinner; I'll grab a bite. Traffic will be lighter after the rush hour."

"I knew this would happen. Drive carefully."

With conscious effort, he avoided Teresa. When she prepared to leave, he summoned the courage to say, "Teresa, I drove in today. Could I drive you home? I'm passing near your apartment anyway. I'd appreciate the company."

His self-control surprised Teresa—that he waited this long. *He wants a repeat performance!* Since the party, his reticence concerning their intimacy puzzled her. She expected him to be all over her, even in the office. Relieved, that their relationship had substance, she said without hesitation, "I'd love to . . . . I hate the subway. Thank you."

That evening started a series of trysts. Phil's job responsibility included maintaining a suite at the Helmsley Hotel™ for visiting company executives and clients. During times of vacancy, he brought Teresa there for extended lunch hours. On those evenings, he was home in time for dinner. On the nights he drove Teresa to her Kew Gardens apartment, he told Margaret that he worked late. This idyllic arrangement lasted until August, the time the baby was due.

Although attentive and considerate toward her, they seldom made love during her pregnancy. He appeared tired and complained about the demands of his job. Margaret sensed the change in Phil.

She verified her suspicions as she removed soiled towels and laundry from the hamper and started the wash. An object fell from Phil's briefs and bounced on the floor. She bent her knees, lowered herself close enough to retrieve an artificial plastic fingernail covered with a shade of nail polish—not hers. When he came home, late again, she confronted him. "Ever since you drive the car to work, you're late two or three times a week. You never worked that much. Are you seeing someone? The truth!"

"Margaret, dearest . . . ."

"Don't Margaret dearest me! No more lies!"

"If you insist—I didn't want to upset you during your pregnancy. It's not you, it's me."

"Don't try that excuse"

"Truthfully, I can't cope with the changes to your body. I loved your smooth flat belly and now look—it's ugly."

"Ugly?"

"You're more of a mother-person. That night at the Marriott™, everything changed for me—I faked my feelings."

"Bastard! It's my fault you can't get it up?"

"No. I love you—but in a different way."

"It's Teresa, isn't it? I knew when you came home with a hickey. You thought I didn't see it."

"She doesn't mean anything to me. It's casual sex."

"The lying continues. Since when is sex ever casual?"

"It's possible to love more than one person. I read a book documenting scientific experiments as proof."

"You can find books to justify all your sins. Do you want a divorce? Do you want to marry her?"

"Certainly not! I love you. I need you and our baby. I won't see her again."

"I don't believe you."

"I'll see a psychiatrist. We'll work things out—for the baby."

After admitting his deceit, Phil was grateful Margaret did not force him to leave and allowed him to sleep in the guest bedroom. In bed alone, thoughts of Phil making love to another woman, tortured Margaret. *Can I ever trust him and love him—as before?* She fell asleep emotionally exhausted, her eyes swollen. Next morning, she awoke with a strange rash on her body. She attributed it to Phil's infidelity.

He called from the office later that day. "I arranged for a consultation this evening with a psychoanalyst, Doctor Reid. I think he can help me." Doctor Reid, about five years younger than Phil, displayed degrees attesting to his recently acquired qualifications. *What life experiences can he possibly have that will help my feelings toward Margaret? I promised her, I would get help.*

"I don't believe you."

"That's the *real* reason I'll be home late."

"Not Teresa?"

"I'll never see Teresa except in a strictly business situation. After all, she is my assistant and I can't avoid her completely. Saving our family is my priority."

*　　*　　*

When he arrived home, Margaret remained cold and aloof. He tried to kiss her; she turned her face. To break the silence he volunteered, "I feel better now."

"I'm glad."

"Doctor Reid explained that my feelings toward you aren't unusual; he resolved similar problems for others."

"I can't trust you."

"I've scheduled weekly appointments."

"To see your whore?"

"Stop that!"

She did not believe him. His voice betrayed his unfaithful act with Teresa. He never told Teresa of Margaret's confrontation and had no intention to change—only to be discrete.

Chapter 8

Except for weekly psychotherapy sessions, Phil arrived home early. He attended to Margaret's needs with gestures of love and an excess of consideration. Exaggerating his concern for her welfare and with frequent declarations of his love, Phil convinced her that the affair ended. His apparent remorse swayed Margaret to overcome her hurt. *How can I remain angry with the father of my child? I need him.*

Impatient to lighten her burden, Margaret welcomed any sign of fruition; she expected the baby the second week of August. Margaret truly believed that Phil returned to his senses and she forgave him for the baby's sake. Assured of her trust, Phil resumed his double life—charmed his way into Margaret's heart and fulfilled his desires with Teresa.

*   *   *

Phil cancelled his session with Doctor Reid and drove Teresa home. He followed her into the apartment and while she perused her mail, started to liberate her from her clothing. She slipped from his grasp laughing, ran into the bathroom and locked the door. She shouted over the sound of running water, "Phil, you're an animal. Give me a chance to get ready." Meanwhile he undressed, turned back the bedcovers and waited.

During their lovemaking, Teresa revealed that she used a voodoo magic potion to entrap him. Since then, he found it convenient to believe the unwilling victim theory . . . captive of a wild passionate witch. He ignored his marriage vows and schemed to arrange time with Teresa. The next day, they met in the company suite during lunch hour for a clandestine love session.

*   *   *

Margaret couldn't sleep; the baby kicked, anxious to arrive. She grabbed Phil's arm . . . awakened him with a start.

"My water broke—I think it's time."

"For what?"

"The baby's coming."

"I'll phone Doctor Barnes."

While Margaret prepared for departure in the bathroom, Phil notified the doctor then called Teresa, waking her. "We're going to Nassau Hospital™. Don't expect me at work tomorrow."

Phil waited at the door with Margaret's coat and the overnight case. "Are you all right?" he asked. They hurried to the car.

Exhilarated, Phil drove through empty roads and ignored stop signs, traffic signals and raced north on Meadowbrook Parkway to Nassau Hospital™ in Mineola. If stopped by police, Margaret's swollen belly provided an excuse. Phil arrived at the hospital Emergency Entrance and assisted Margaret from the car. A nurse's aide placed Margaret in a wheelchair and pushed her toward obstetrics while Phil completed the admitting process.

Margaret winced with frequent intense contractions. Her obvious distress unnerved Phil. He made futile attempts to distract her. She would not listen.

"I love you and only you. This baby is proof of our love."

Margaret's contractions eased. During a lull in the one-sided conversation Phil asked, "Do you think I could get a cup of coffee? I'll be gone only a minute, dear."

"Go. I'll be fine."

Phil took the elevator to the ground floor coffee vending machines. The door opened with a view of the waiting area. Teresa rose from a chair and hurried toward him. She greeted him with a tender embrace.

"I couldn't let you go through this alone."

Dumbfounded by her presence, Phil said, "Would you like a cup of coffee? I have to return; Margaret's in labor."

"I understand. I'll be waiting. Go—she needs you."

He remained oblivious of Teresa's devious intent to posses him—her determination to use him to fulfill her life. The birth of his child would not interfere.

*   *   *

Margaret's anxiety increased with every pain.

"Have a sip?" He offered the cup to her.

"It wouldn't be good for the baby. I'm glad you're here."

In the Delivery Room, Phil encouraged Margaret. "You can do it, dear. Soon you'll hold our baby. You can do it!"

"Shut up!" She shouted. "You don't know . . . I'd like to see you do it!"

Previously, Phil had patiently listened while fathers gave detailed accounts of witnessing the birth of their children and described the bonding that ensued from the shared experience. He thought something was wrong with him for abhorring the entire process. There's no joy in the reality of childbirth. When he saw the baby's head emerge, he could not perceive ever feeling a sexual desire for Margaret. *Why did she have to get pregnant? How can she be elated at the sight of the messy infant with the severed umbilical cord? She ruined everything!*

*   *   *

In the waiting room, Teresa leafed through outdated magazines. Jealous of Phil's concern and anxious for him to return, she looked toward the elevator whenever the doors opened. When he did appear, he glanced in her direction and signaled with his hands for her to remain seated and shaking his head side to side mouthed, "NO!" He passed her without acknowledging her presence and as he approached a group of people he announced, "It's a boy. They're both doing well." He embraced the woman and shook hands with the man. "I'll take you to Margaret and your new grandson." *These are Margaret's parents and sisters!*

Phil accompanied them into the elevator and to the nursery. Through the window, he proudly pointed to his sleeping son. Then he returned to Margaret's side. "Our son is beautiful. You need sleep, so I'll go home and return later." He kissed her cheek. "I love you and our baby. Do you need anything?"

She shook her head. "No, I don't think so."

"Then I'll see you later."

Phil's sudden departure surprised Margaret's parents.

When Phil emerged from the elevator, Teresa rushed toward him. "Congratulations on the birth of your son. I'm so happy for you." Her scent, in sharp contrast to the hospital odors, reminded him of their shared intimacy. They left in his car. On the drive to Merrick, their silence betrayed their thoughts. Perhaps a sense of guilt enhanced anticipated pleasure.

Since neighbors are rarely awake that early, Phil hoped no one observed them. He quickly ushered Teresa into the house—the home he and Margaret shared.

Teresa's eyes glistened with the opulent furnishings. The white marble tiled foyer opened into a living room with white carpeting and furniture of soft white leather. She followed Phil upstairs to a sitting room with overstuffed chairs, sofa; and a television with sound system that filled one wall. On the left, the master bedroom with walk-in closet adjoined a bedroom converted into a nursery. Through the open doorway, Teresa saw the baby's crib.

A large arch formed an alcove with mirrored walls with an ornate table for Margaret's cosmetics. Along one wall, twin washbowls and a mirrored cabinet reflected light from the skylight. Beyond the alcove, the bathtub set in rose-colored marble dominated the master bathroom. A partition discretely separated the commode and bidet from the main room, while intricately engraved doors enclosed the shower.

"You have a beautiful, home, Phil."

"Excuse me while I shower after my all-night ordeal at the hospital."

Teresa turned the television on at low volume. She undressed. Passing through the alcove, she walked through a mist of Margaret's perfume and appraised herself in Margaret's mirror. Phil's back was toward her when she opened the shower doors and stepped in. She pressed her breasts against his back; her arms encircled his waist. She reached downward—he gasped at her touch. She lathered his genitals until; unable to wait, he turned and carried her dripping wet into Margaret's bed.

Hospital visiting hours were over, when they awoke in each other's arms—the baby's room in full view.

*   *   *

The maternity ward is usually a happy place filled with smiling parents and awed siblings carrying balloons, stuffed toys, flowers and candy. Other wards fight sickness and death, the maternity section celebrates the beginning of new life. In incubators, premature infants attached to plastic tubing and electronic sensors struggle to survive, while worried parents smile and gesture encouragement through glass windows.

That afternoon Margaret's parents and friends brought gifts. She watched the door for Phil's arrival, her disappointment evident. *Why wasn't he here? He must have fallen asleep and didn't awaken in time for visiting hours.* She phoned home . . . no answer. *Where is he?*

Phil arrived fifteen minutes before evening visiting hours ended. He held a novelty foot-long cigar encircled with a blue band imprinted 'It's a Boy!' He gave Margaret a bouquet of white flowers tinted blue and a box of chocolates. Acting the clown, he said, "I'm a father! I can't believe I'm a father! Thank you Margaret!"

"Have you seen our son?

"He's bald—with the face of a little old man."

"All newborns fill out in time. How can you say he looks like an old man? He's beautiful."

"He's the only one with no hair."

"Because he's special."

Unable to determine whether he was serious or clowning, she wished he stayed home. *Something about his behavior isn't right!* Professing his gratitude and undying love, he kissed her outstretched hand. She accepted his apology and his excuses for missing afternoon visiting hours. Yet, she doubted his sincerity.

Visiting hours ended; all left except Phil. He remained until the floor nurse threatened to call security. In truth, he hated hospitals. When he left, Margaret felt drained, physically and emotionally.

The nurse gave baby Mathew to Margaret who gently guided his eager mouth to her moist breast. His pleasurable rhythmic sucking calmed her; a sense of peace and the warmth helped ease her premonitions.

* * *

Teresa approached Phil as he stepped from the elevator.

"I saw your baby in the nursery. He's beautiful. Someday, we'll have our own . . . ."

"Why complicate our lives? I have enough to deal with."

On the way to Merrick, Teresa sat beside him in silence. *Will I ever bear his child?*

At the house, a cocktail helped dispel thoughts of Margaret, the baby and Phil's reaction. Cuddled in Margaret's bed Teresa said, "You're lucky to have me take care of you. Otherwise you'd be lying here alone."

* * *

On the second day of Margaret's hospital confinement, Phil hired a woman, unacquainted with Margaret, to change the bed sheets and pillowcases, do laundry, and vacuum thoroughly to remove any trace of his betrayal. Then, after packing a change of shirts and underwear, he drove to work. To insure the house stayed clean, he planned to sleep at Teresa's apartment during Margaret's absence.

From his office, he called New York Telephone™ and ordered call forwarding after four rings—to transfer all calls from his home to Teresa's apartment. If Margaret phoned during the night, he could answer without arousing suspicion. The opportunity for duplicity stimulated him. The challenge of infidelity without retribution fueled his sexual fantasies. *Imagine lying in bed with Teresa, while I talk to Margaret. What a turn on!*

Chapter 9

Intermittent fevers extended Margaret's recovery from childbirth to five days. On her last night in the hospital, Margaret phoned Phil. Unknown to her, Phil answered the phone in Teresa's apartment.

"Hi! How are you managing without me?" Margaret's cheerful greeting caught him off guard.

"You don't know how much I miss you."

"We can leave in the morning. Can you be here at eleven?"

"I'll come earlier. Home isn't the same without you. I missed you terribly. I love you."

"I love you, too."

Phil's words angered Teresa. *How can he lie to her with me beside him? Is he lying to me?*

Rather than turn away from him, she intensified their sexual passion in order to delay him.

*   *   *

After breakfast at a diner on Queens Boulevard, Phil drove Teresa to work. Returning from Manhattan, he stopped at a florist to buy flowers for Margaret and a stuffed toy for Matthew. In the hospital cafeteria, he drank a mug of strong black coffee before facing Margaret.

Relieved to shed her robe and nightgown, Margaret unable to close the zipper on her skirt, asked the nurse for a safety pin. She readied the baby's clothing, a white sweater and hat trimmed with blue ribbon and spread out the blanket. When the nurse brought little Matthew, Margaret stripped him of all hospital attire. Matthew kicked and stretched his tiny legs with newfound freedom. She laughed at his futile attempts to avoid her grasp and his aversion to clothing. *At last, I will care for my baby at home—in his own room.*

Phil cleared their release at the cashier's office. Margaret and Matthew were dressed and anxious to leave. He kissed her cheek and the baby's forehead. "Are you ready?"

"Ready. I can't wait to sleep in my own bed—cook my own food."

The nurse's aide brought a wheelchair for mother and baby.

"I don't need that. I can manage."

"It's hospital rules. At the main entrance, you're on your own."

Phil preceded them to his car, parked in a restricted zone of the driveway. With exaggerated concern, he helped Margaret from the wheelchair. Despite protests, he placed a generous tip into the aide's pocket.

*   *   *

During the drive home, Phil feared missing any clue that might arouse suspicion despite his precautions to eliminate any trace of Teresa. He felt guilty, yet justified. All he heard during the pregnancy was, "The baby kicked. Feel—I think it has the hiccups." *Having a child became the center of Margaret's universe. I have needs, too. Teresa understands me; we're good for each other. I still love Margaret but in a different way.* He was jealous of Matthew—the way Margaret cuddled and talked to the baby—caressed and played with him—fulfilled every want . . . *any wonder that I turned to Teresa?*

They settled into their new way of life; Matthew took over the house. When Matthew slept, Margaret exercised to attain her former figure. Phil worked long hours to avoid time at home. Margaret never questioned his absence. Always loving and attentive, he frequently brought gifts and flowers. In November, they resumed sexual intercourse within a charged atmosphere; Margaret suspected his affair with Teresa continued despite his denials. He even came home early and sober from the Christmas party. When the descending ball in Times Square announced the New Year, they toasted with champagne in front of the television. Phil was content with his double life. *I love two beautiful women, and each satisfies my desires in their own way.*

Juggling his affection between Margaret and Teresa challenged Phil. Once he justified his behavior, his conscience didn't stand a chance. He took pride in his sexual prowess; the same night he left Teresa's bed, he went home for sex with Margaret while pretending she was Teresa. This feat substantiated his virility; his lust knew no bounds. Since Matthew started on formula, Margaret's body returned to its former shape and Phil's impotence disappeared. *How long can I continue to satisfy both women?*

Valentine's Day created a problem. *How can I share myself?* Phil shopped for gifts for his loves; identical articles of lingerie and Obsession™, each separately gift-wrapped. To lull Margaret into a sense of security he said, "Tomorrow's Valentine's Day. Arrange for a baby-sitter and meet me in Manhattan for a night on the town? You need a diversion."

"What have you planned?"

He had not planned anything and completely ignored her question.

Margaret, pleased with the prospect, hated to leave Matthew. Phil sensed her anxiety.

"I'll phone often to check on Matthew."

*   *   *

Teresa worked late on Valentine's Day while Phil waited for Margaret in his office. He convinced Teresa earlier, that if they were to continue their affair, this date with Margaret was necessary. Curious if Margaret gained weight, Teresa greeted her in a nonchalant manner. "Good evening, Mrs. Noble. How is the baby?"

"He's doing quite well. Every day brings new progress."

Teresa seethed—powerless. *How can he torture me this way?*

Margaret looked fabulous; if anything, motherhood improved her appearance. She walked into Phil's office and removed her jacket, revealing her newly acquired figure. She wore a form-fitting navy blue beaded dress with sparkling sequins; the low neckline and diamond drop pendant accented her cleavage. Phil rose from his chair and before he could say anything, she kissed him—long and lingering for Teresa's benefit. Watching them through the open door, Teresa felt a distinct disadvantage against formidable opposition; her petite body lacked Margaret's elegance and poise. She didn't own expensive fashionable clothing. Yet, Teresa never wavered; she vowed to destroy the marriage and eventually marry Phil.

Before Margaret's arrival, Phil instructed Teresa to make a reservation at the Rainbow Room™. *He never takes me there! He rarely takes me anywhere, except to bed—not that I don't enjoy those occasions. It's time he treated me with consideration after all the pleasure I've given him.*

She watched Phil give Margaret the gifts. Margaret opened the perfume and dabbed her neck. Then she opened the lingerie, and held it in front of herself. "Are you sure you want to go? I know where your mind is."

On the verge of tears, Teresa overheard and hastily decided to leave. She called out, "Goodnight Mr. and Mrs. Noble." Her voice choked, unable to say more as she entered the elevator.

*   *   *

He opened the apartment door; a vase narrowly missed his head and crashed on hallway's marble floor.

"Are you crazy? You could have killed me."

"I should have! You still love her!"

"I thought you understood. I did what I had to do—for us."

"I don't believe you."

"Would I trouble with Valentine's Day gifts if I didn't love you?"

Reluctant to change her mood, she tore open the wrappings. When she saw the identical lingerie Phil had given Margaret, she threw it at him.

"Keep this! Do you expect me to be Margaret? She wore it for you last night!"

"Believe me. It's folded in her dresser drawer."

"I'm sorry, but it's difficult knowing you are with Margaret. Would you like a drink? Help yourself. Give me a minute to freshen up." *Maybe he's right. If I continue this jealous behavior, I may lose him. I can pretend to believe.*

Phil poured a scotch and soda. After adding ice cubes, he waited.

Teresa appeared in flimsy lingerie . . . walked toward him with outstretched arms. He nearly choked on a piece of ice when she straddled his knees and leaned forward to nibble on his neck and face, and then hungrily kissed his lips. *The time for words passed; the time for action arrived.*

*   *   *

That morning, Margaret planned to shop for clothes at Saks Fifth Avenue™ and Lord and Taylor™, a pleasure she was unable to enjoy during her pregnancy. She left six-month old Matthew at her mother's house. Matthew renewed grandma's skills in feeding and changing babies, an art grandma joyfully abandoned when her children outgrew that stage.

When Margaret returned, mother prepared a light dinner and tea while Margaret displayed her bargains. Matthew, bored with the whole process, deprived of his nap, fretted, and cried lustily. In her haste to leave, Margaret neglected to pack the Matthew's pacifier, the only one that quieted him. She belatedly discovered the oversight as she tucked him in his crib.

Margaret phoned Phil's office to ask him to drive by her mother's house for the pacifier. The receptionist said, "I'm sorry. Mr. Noble isn't available."

"Can you reach him or take a message? This is his wife. It's important!"

"I'm afraid he's gone for the day. He left no reach number."

"Thank you." *I know where he is.*

She arrived at her mother's home and rang the doorbell repeatedly. Margaret handed Matthew to her. Surprised, her mother asked, "What's wrong?"

"Trust me, Mom. I know what I'm doing. Watch the baby and give me your car."

"Where are you going?"

"I'll tell you everything when I return. I love you, Mom."

"Drive carefully."

She did not want to alert Phil by driving her car. Margaret knew Teresa's address from her Christmas card list. While hunting for a parking space, she found Phil's car. Infuriated by his lies and her trust in him, she pressed buttons at the entrance until someone buzzed her in. Rather than wait for the elevator she took the stairs to Teresa's apartment and pounded on the door.

"I want to speak to my husband."

"Margaret?"

"I know he's with you."

"He isn't here."

"Open the door now or I'll let everyone in the building know you're a whore."

The door opened slightly. Teresa, wrapped in a robe, said, "Mrs. Noble—he's not here. I swear."

"You're a liar!" Margaret forced her way in.

Phil stood, bare-footed and shirtless, zipping his trousers. "You lying bastard! How could you . . . ? You swore this was finished. All those sweet words last night—I believed you." She wanted to hit him with her fists, except that required physical contact. He stood in silence. Margaret turned to Teresa, "He's married and a new father, but you don't care." She left shouting, "I hope you'll be very happy together. You deserve each other!"

Chapter 10

Losing Phil after seven years of marriage horrified Margaret. *I would deprive Matthew of his father. Yet, how can I live with his deceit? I owe Matthew a chance. Can I reconcile? Teresa wanted me to discover their continuing affair. That explains his late work nights, excuses, tiredness, and unexpected gifts. How could he . . . after all his promises?*

As a child when she bruised her knee she didn't cry until her mother could soothe her; she now held back the tears until mother opened the door. Then Margaret, like a heartbroken child, told her story between sobs.

Meanwhile, Phil hastily dressed, then ran to his car to pursue Margaret . . . explain and apologize. He feared this time Margaret wouldn't forgive him; he surpassed the limit of her patience. He drove to Merrick and not finding her at home phoned Margaret's mother. "Is my wife there?"

"She doesn't wish to speak to you."

"Tell her I'm coming over."

"I don't want you in my house! She doesn't want to see you!"

"I'm coming anyway."

Phil hung up the phone, relieved that she arrived safely at her mother's . . . .

*　　*　　*

Margaret's sisters were leaving for Copperfield's™, a local disco, when mother said, "You're angry but I won't permit you to mope. Go with them. Matthew's fine with me."

"My eyes are swollen; my face is a mess."

"Cold water and cosmetics work wonders."

Her sister said, "We'll wait. Come with us."

"You're sure?

"You're wasting time. We'll wait for you."

* * *

When Phil arrived, he confronted mother. "I want to see my wife."

"She's not here."

"I'll wait until she returns. We have to talk."

"Then stay out of sight. You disgust me—the way you treat her."

Phil entered the living room stretched out on the Oriental rug and waited in silence.

The tension hung like a dark cloud. Matthew slept throughout and mother manufactured tasks to keep busy. Phil didn't dare move from the living room rug. The interminable wait ended when Margaret returned in a happy mood. Before becoming aware of Phil's presence, she blurted, "I met someone I could talk to—straightforward and honest. His name is David. He's not at all like Phil."

Phil stood up and startled her.

"What are you doing here? You belong with your little friend."

"Margaret, I love you!"

"Go to her and leave me alone. I've had enough of your lies!"

"Please—talk to me!"

He burst into tears, an act worthy of the Academy Award®, and on his knees pleaded for another chance. She fought an impulse to console him in his piteous state. Instead, she turned away.

"I made a mistake! It will never happen again. I'll do anything for another chance."

"How can I trust you? You lie without qualms. When I feel secure, you give me reason to doubt."

"I'll resume therapy with Doctor Reid. I'll get counseling from the parish priest. I'll do whatever it takes . . . ."

"What about Teresa?"

"I'll transfer her to another department. She won't work for me."

"Can I believe you?"

"I'll prove I love you. She placed me under some kind of a voodoo spell. I swear I couldn't help myself."

"You're lying again!"

"It's the truth—she admitted it."

"The man who's always in control—helpless? That's why I can't believe you."

A cry from Matthew signaled a truce. Margaret picked him up, cooing, "We're going home, baby. It's past your bedtime. Daddy will follow."

As Phil moved his personal items and clothing from the master bedroom into the guest room. Margaret said, "I can't live in a one-sided marriage."

*   *   *

Margaret doubted whether he could refrain from lying even to the psychotherapist. Patient confidentiality worked in Phil's favor. After a month of weekly sessions, she phoned Dr. Reid.

"This is Mrs. Noble, my husband Phil is your patient. How is he progressing?"

"You know I can't answer that. Our sessions are confidential."

"Tell me; is he sick or putting on an act? That's all I ask."

"Your husband is a sick man with self-destructive tendencies. I can't reveal more."

"Thank you doctor."

The next day Margaret went with Matthew to the library and selected books on psychology to research self-destructive tendencies. *If he is sick, perhaps I can help him recover and save my marriage.*

*   *   *

Phil appeared sincere in his resolve. At his first meeting with Father Wrobleski, the Catholic parish priest, Phil explained his need for counseling. Father offered him a glass of wine to ease his discomfort. Phil made a mental note of the label. He brought a bottle to every subsequent meeting. Through the sacrament of Penance, Phil confessed his sins and promised to never again yield to temptation—another lie. *If only Margaret forgave me as easily as the priest.* The counseling sessions turned into social visits.

*   *   *

On Monday morning, Teresa, curious after Margaret's confrontation outside the apartment, anxiously waited for Phil. He forced a smile. "Good morning, Teresa. I'm sorry for my abrupt departure."

"It was embarrassing—her calling me a whore. I love you—there's a difference."

"But it happened. I promised to transfer you to another department. You'll work for Mr. Brent—at an increased salary."

"I'm not a whore! Don't try to buy me!"

"It's to our advantage—at least until I get a legal separation."

Teresa's spirits immediately rose. *He intends to leave Margaret!*

"For appearances we need to be discreet. Otherwise Margaret will clean me out financially in a divorce settlement."

"It will be difficult, but I'm willing to sacrifice for our future."

Teresa, ecstatic at hearing the word 'divorce', tried to hide her enthusiasm. *Phil made a commitment—an engagement without the ring. Can I believe him? Or is he lying to me? I'll have to chance it.*

"What are you doing for lunch?"

Her heart leaped at the prospect of celebrating in the suite at the Helmsley™. She knew exactly what she would be doing for lunch.

*   *   *

Events accelerated Phil's decision to marry Teresa. He loved both women, in different ways. The complexities of a double life challenged him more than he expected. Although fun for a while, he couldn't keep track of his lies. With frazzled nerves, he could not concentrate on his work and longed for a more tranquil life. He felt tired . . . used. If he truly loved Margaret, he would have resisted involvement with Teresa. Apparently, their marriage lacked something. In the early days filled with discovery and passion, he lost himself in Margaret's love. Their marital trouble started with her pregnancy. He loved Matthew, but babies failed to interest him; perhaps when Matthew is older they will have more in common. *What can I do with an infant? Matthew is Margaret's little toy.*

Teresa fulfilled every fantasy. Although at times demanding, she was definitely passionate, loving, and completely attentive to him. His needs came first; she made him feel alive. Until 'divorce' passed his lips, he never intended to leave Margaret. *How will I have the nerve to tell her?*

*   *   *

That evening at his counseling session with Father Wrobleski, Phil revealed his decision. He asked the priest for advice on sparing Margaret's feelings. Father Wrobleski, inadequate as Phil's counselor, attempted to salvage the marriage.

"The Catholic religion does not recognize divorce. With a child involved, annulment is impossible. Have you seriously tried?"

"I have Father. However, she banished me to the guest room. She refuses to listen."

"My prayers are with you. Please reconsider."

"I have. It's no use."

From his bookshelf of inspirational reading, the priest removed a book on the sanctity of marriage and its responsibilities." Phil, I'm sorry your marriage failed. Go somewhere secluded—meditate and read this book. Get in touch with your true inner feelings without distraction. With God's help you'll find the answer."

"Thanks for listening. I give you credit; celibacy has its advantages. Sharing my problems helped. Your advice makes sense."

Phil succeeded in transferring his dilemma to Father Wrobleski and sharing the blame for his doomed marriage.

* * *

At Margaret's insistence, Phil continued to sleep in the guest room. His docility puzzled her; *he should have insisted on sex by now, unless . . . .* One evening Margaret confronted him. "You're still seeing her. Aren't you?"

"What are you saying? It's finished! I'll prove it."

He dialed Teresa's number. "Hello? Teresa? I hope you'll forgive me—but our relationship is over."

Margaret listened on the extension phone to insure he called Teresa. Since he could not warn Teresa of his bluff, she thought he meant it.

"What do you mean—it's over? How can you treat me this way? I love you more than life—I'd rather die than lose you!"

Alarmed at her reaction, he shouted, "Don't do anything foolish!"

"If I die, it'll be on your conscience,"

He heard the phone hit the floor.

"Teresa. I didn't mean it. Wait. I'm coming over."

After his sudden rejection, she grabbed a bottle of sleeping pills from the medicine cabinet and swallowed the contents with water, then lay in a fetal position on the bathroom floor waiting for oblivion.

Phil turned to Margaret. "She's crazy! She's going to kill herself and it's my fault. I've got to stop her!"

Margaret feeling partial responsibility, called the teen-aged girl next door to stay with Matthew as Phil started the car. They raced to Kew Gardens fearing the worst.

Phil knocked on the apartment door. *If only I had warned Teresa, she would have played along. I never thought she would believe me.*

He used his key to the apartment. Teresa lay on the bathroom floor with an empty bottle of prescription sleeping pills. He felt her neck for a pulse and checked for breathing. Rather than wait for an ambulance, Phil shouted to Margaret, "Bring the pill container." Then he wrapped Teresa in a robe and carried her to the car. Margaret tended to her in the back seat in a futile attempt to awaken her. At the Elmhurst General™ emergency entrance, Phil shouted for assistance. When apprised of her overdose the doctor pumped her stomach and began intravenous.

Phil was frightened. *What have I done? Teresa is in serious condition because of me! How would Teresa react if I abandoned her? If she recovers, I will make it up to her.* With remorse for his actions, he dragged Margaret into a situation she did not deserve.

*   *   *

Two weeks after Teresa's suicide attempt and her release from the hospital, Phil informed Margaret that Father Wrobleski recommended a weekend retreat to seek God's guidance. Showing her the book, he said, "You can read this when I return." Margaret did not oppose his absence.

"Where do you plan to go?"

"I'm not telling anyone, except Father Wrobleski. I need time to meditate undisturbed. Only in emergency will he call me."

"How do I reach him?"

"I'll leave his number by the phone."

Margaret agreed, heartened by his effort to change.

The following day Phil met Teresa at lunch. "I have good news. On Friday, pack a bag for the weekend. Make sure to include warm clothing, early March can be very cold at the Mount Airy Lodge™."

"Are you serious? What did you tell Margaret?"

"Never mind. This weekend is ours."

*   *   *

Margaret pleased at Phil's positive action, helped pack his suitcase. Friday morning, Margaret prepared a breakfast of hot pancakes with maple syrup and steaming coffee.

"Truthfully, I'll miss you. Please make the most of this retreat. I'm grateful for Father Wrobleski's help."

"His number is by the phone."

"I won't disturb you, but please call, so I'll know you're OK."

"I'll probably leave work at noon to beat the traffic. I'm taking Monday off. I should be home sometime after noon. I love you. Say a prayer for me."

As he drove away, Margaret hoped their rift would mend.

*   *   *

Bubbling with enthusiasm, Teresa arrived at work with luggage. *How had Phil arranged the get-away? Did he tell Margaret he wanted a divorce?* Mister Brent granted her request for time off for a ski weekend.

At noon, she met Phil waiting curbside in his car. She placed her luggage on the rear seat and slid in the front . . . . She leaned over to kiss him.

"Save it for later, dear. Let's go before someone sees us. You know office gossip."

*   *   *

The grandeur of Mount Airy Lodge™ impressed Teresa. The clientele mostly couples here for skiing and romance, not necessarily in that order, provided a friendly atmosphere. Phil registered and signaled the bellhop. They followed him to the suite. He placed their luggage on folding stands and explained the thermostat settings. "It gets pretty cold in here."

Teresa thought *not if I can help it*. Together with a whole weekend ahead, she controlled her impulse to embrace Phil and guide him to the bed. *I'll show a degree of refinement—pique his interest—tease him and then drive him crazy.* She avoided his grasp. "I have to freshen up before dinner, I'm hungry. In our haste we skipped lunch." Phil's thoughts weren't on food.

In the dining room, a corsage of red rose buds was beside Teresa's plate. "How lovely . . ."

The waiter poured champagne; Phil raised his glass, "To Father Wrobleski. Thank you for this weekend and your excellent counseling."

After a leisurely dinner, they strolled around the complex. In one large room, flames from the fireplace cast flickering lights on the walls with welcoming warmth. Outside, the new-fallen snow reflected pale moonlight. A slight shiver passed through Teresa, as they stood gazing through the picture window at the icy slopes. Phil placed his arm around her, "Are you cold?" He picked up the house phone and arranged to have the fireplace in their suite ready to welcome them. They stopped at the lounge for a nightcap. Teresa was in heaven. Without fear of discovery, their love took on a new dimension. The luxury of time was theirs. The sexual frenzy to possess each other changed into a relaxed desire.

In a normal situation, normal for them, they showered together—this time each bathed alone in anticipation. Phil, in his robe, waited on the sofa before a roaring fire. His heart quickened at the sight of her petite figure in a flowing white peignoir, silhouetted by the dancing flames. Slowly, she approached—the outline of her breasts teased him. She sat beside him—he leaned toward her—she moved away.

"Let's talk awhile."

"Why waste time?"

"Are you divorcing Margaret to marry me?"

"Teresa, you doubt me? Haven't I shown my love for you? We'll marry—only it will take time."

"What do I have that Margaret hasn't?"

"You're completely different. I thought I loved Margaret, my first love—we were young. After a whirlwind courtship, I married the perfect homemaker; she let me assume control. I should have known it was an act. The first time that she contradicted me—our first argument was the day before our wedding. It was unusually hot and I wanted to go to Jones Beach. She said, 'I will not walk down the aisle with a sunburned face and peeling nose.' I said that I was going anyway and started to drive away she threw our engagement ring in the street and screamed 'You can forget the marriage—keep your ring!' I stopped the car, picked up the ring and left. In the evening, I returned with a bouquet of roses and a sincere apology, which she accepted."

"After her display of temper, why did you follow through with the wedding?"

"I loved her strawberry blond hair, ready smile and fabulous figure. Besides, she is intelligent and charming. I'm a determined person; she challenged me."

"Do you still love her?"

"I have feelings . . . ."

"At first she asked my opinion on everything, the apartment, the furniture, even the breed of dog we should adopt. She agreed with every decision I made. For two years I flourished. Then without my knowledge, after saving enough money for a down payment, she met with a realtor and placed a binder on the house in Merrick—without consulting me. After working all day, I walked into the apartment to find her in her coat and holding the car keys. She drove to the house in Merrick. She said, 'I wanted to surprise you. What do you think?' I asked her 'Whose house is this?' 'It's ours!' A chill went through my body accompanied by an indescribable weakness. I physically trembled and didn't want to leave the car. Suddenly, I felt a childlike helplessness trapped in an untenable situation. In my lifetime, I never lost self-control. This house, a symbol of the permanent nature of our marriage, made me wonder what I have gotten into."

Teresa responded with sympathy. "Our marriage can be different. With an open marriage, there is no reason to feel trapped. We can be our own person and still love each other. A wedding ring isn't necessary to seal our love."

She slowly opened his robe and placed her cheek against his flesh. Together they slid off the sofa to the thick carpet. The burning logs in the fireplace filled the room with dancing shadows. This was the first time they weren't on each other in lustful frenzy.

As they lie in front of the fire, t, safe from interruption, Phil proceeded gently. He pulled the thick comforter from the bed; the bristly carpet irritated his skin. In a playful mood, he spread the comforter on the floor and rolled her on it. Limp as a rag doll, unlike her usual aggressiveness, she lie face down, awaiting his next move, He inched her silk nightgown upward, alternately caressing the backs of her legs with his fingers. His lips followed the direction of her gown toward the satin curves of her back that glowed orange from light of the flames. When the nightgown bunched around her neck, he stopped—turned her to face him and removed the filmy material over her head. He continued his caresses and kisses down the length of her body ending at her toes. She waited motionless, wishing this weekend would last forever. When he removed his robe, the invigorating contrast rejuvenated him; one side of his body felt the heat, the other side a chill.

*　　*　　*

Between ice-skating, swimming, indoor tennis and social activities they managed time for love. After a Sunday afternoon rest, Teresa started to dress for dinner. Phil said, "Honey, I'm taking the car to gas up for an early start."

"Can't that wait until morning?

"The service station might not be open. I won't be long."

To Phil's relief, the snowplow cleared and sanded the road, lined on each side by two-foot snow banks. The falling snow limited his vision. While the attendant pumped gasoline and cleared the windshield, Phil walked to an outdoor phone booth. Kicking the snow away from the folding door, he forced it open. The snow prevented the door from closing completely and block out the chilling wind. Phil removed the glove from his right hand and dialed Margaret's number. The dial stuck with the cold and he forced it to return—he hoped to get the right number and not have to repeat the process. *Answer Margaret—I know you are there.*

"Hello? Phil?"

He shouted over the sound of the wind. "Hi. I think of you all weekend. How's Matthew?"

"We're fine. How's the retreat?"

"I miss you both.

The relentless wind whistled through the partially open door. Margaret asked, "What's that sound?"

"It's cold here and snowing. I'd better hang up before I freeze to death. I love you."

"We pray for you every night. 'Bye"

Phil paid the attendant and drove back to Teresa. "With this heavy snow we'll be lucky to leave in the morning."

"I wouldn't mind; I love it here."

*　　*　　*

After Phil's call and tending to Matthew, Margaret lay on her bed. *Why didn't he phone sooner if he was truly concerned? Perhaps I'm overly suspicious.*

By the glow of the night-light, careful not to awaken Matthew, she searched through the drawer of the end table. *It's here—Father Wrobleski's book. Why didn't he phone from the warmth of his room? Why call from an outdoor phone booth in the freezing cold—unless he didn't want some one to hear? Teresa!*

Frustrated, she wanted to kill him. *Only Father Wrobleski knew where they were. I'll not burden the priest with my problems.* Sleep eluded her, tortured by visions of her husband with Teresa. *Is he truly sincere in his desire for reconciliation? Did he accidentally forget the book? No—more likely, the book never interested him; it was merely a clever device to show his sincerity.* Thoughts of previous deceptions haunted her. In the morning, she knew what she must do.

*   *   *

Before leaving on his retreat, Phil promised to return late Monday. Margaret awakened early, fed Matthew and nervously drank her coffee while watching the time. At nine o'clock, she phoned Mr. Brent's office, the receptionist answered. Margaret asked, "Teresa McCormick, please."

"She's not in yet."

Margaret lied, "This is her mother—are you certain?"

"She's on vacation. She will be back tomorrow. Do you wish to leave a message?"

"No—thank you."

He could not have hurt her more if he used physical force. *I loved him, wanted our marriage to work. I forgave him repeatedly. If I confront him, he will go into his sorry act.* She imagined him saying, *"I've been a bad boy. I'm sorry. Please forgive me. I'll never do it again."* It was an act repeated since childhood. *This time I'll play along and pretend I don't suspect anything—see how far he'll go, before I throw him out.*

*   *   *

Teresa dawdled as she packed her luggage. *Thanks to Mama Louise's love potion, Phil made a commitment to marry me . . . a true engagement but without the ring. In addition, I still have today . . . .*

Teresa snuggled beside him, while he silently drove, alert for icy spots although the plows did an excellent job clearing the roads. New-fallen snow covered the landscape with a purity that signified the new aspect of their relationship that began with his oblique marriage proposal.

"Have you told Margaret?"

"About what?"

"About us, Silly! About the divorce."

"I will—in time."

"I'm anxious to become your wife."

"Patience is a virtue. Is it possible for you to be virtuous?"

"I doubt it. Not after this weekend."

He switched the radio to 1010 WINS™ for a rundown of weather and road conditions, putting an end to the conversation. Teresa dozed off, lulled by the motion of the car and the warmth of the heater.

At Teresa's apartment, Phil dashed to the bathroom after the long drive. After splashing cold water on his face, he looked for telltale traces of lipstick. Then he returned to Teresa and attempted to leave.

"It's early afternoon—no need to rush home. Stay awhile."

"I'd love to, but I can't."

"Why not? You could have been stuck in traffic."

". . . only for awhile."

His resolve weakened. He instinctively knew her intentions.

*   *   *

That evening, Phil arrived home as if nothing extraordinary happened. Margaret prepared Matthew for bed as Phil came from behind and kissed the back of her neck; she kept her composure.

"How was your weekend?"

"I feel rejuvenated. The peace and solitude of the countryside gave me the opportunity to meditate and find my way."

"Did you read Father Wrobleski's book?"

"From cover to cover. The author has amazing insight on marriage and relationships. I'll change into comfortable clothes and we'll talk." *The book! Where is it? I haven't seen it! I must have left it in bedroom end table.* It lay undisturbed in the back corner of the drawer. He placed it in his suitcase.

After Phil changed, he lifted Matthew up high. "How's my big boy, today?"

"I'll give you two a little playtime. He's too excited to sleep now. Have you any laundry or clothes for the cleaner?"

"Most likely."

While they played, Margaret unpacked Phil's luggage. To her surprise, she discovered Father Wrobleski's book. *Another of Phil's tricks! Could there be two of them?* She furtively opened the night table drawer. *The book is missing!*

Lying in bed, Phil described the lodge, the quiet nights, the view of the snow-covered slopes as seen through the large picture windows, and in the morning, the magical renewal of the scene by new-fallen snow on the tree branches. He told her about hours spent in meditation and inspirational reading before the crackling wood and the welcome warmth from the fireplace—about his constant thoughts of her and Matthew and about the exhausting drive home. He held her—luxuriating in the scent of her nearness, yet made no move to initiate sex. Margaret knew why.

Phil swore that the retreat changed him—that Teresa was completely out of his life—that the therapy and counseling yielded excellent results. Margaret's instinct warned her otherwise.

*   *   *

Phil and Jack Brent, an associate, scheduled a 9:00am conference in Chicago. Phil told Margaret they were leaving Sunday afternoon to prepare for the meeting and get a night's rest. Margaret offered to drive him to LaGuardia airport, but since a business account covered expenses, he insisted on a cab.

After he left, Margaret gathered a bundle of clothing for the dry-cleaner. When she checked the pockets of one of his suits, she found slip of paper, a note in Phil's handwriting. 'Meet Jack at LaGuardia, Monday 8:00am, American Airlines™ 9:00am Flight.' She was furious. *Phil left for the airport the day before the conference! He plans a night with Teresa before leaving.*

Early on Monday, Margaret dressed the sleepy Matthew and secured him safely in his car seat. She drove to Kew Gardens, parked near the entrance to Teresa's building and waited. About seven o'clock, a cab arrived. Margaret watched Phil emerge from the building and carry his luggage to the rear of the cab. As the driver opened the trunk, Margaret drove slowly past, sounded the horn and waved her hand to Phil. His startled expression when he recognized her and the car signified the end of their marriage.

Margaret faced the heart-rending reality that Phil would never change. She couldn't live in a deceitful marriage. *I don't deserve this treatment; I caught him again, making a fool of me. Although it breaks my heart, this is the end of our marriage.* Angry and disgusted she drove home—stress turned into resolve.

At home, she placed Matthew in the playpen; and then removed Phil's clothes from the closet and dumped them on the foyer floor. She packed the contents of his armoire and personal toiletries into cardboard cartons. *He'll get no more chances.*

*   *   *

When he phoned, Margaret refused to speak to him. Phil arrived by airport service limo at his front door. He expected a strained welcome after she discovered him leaving Teresa's apartment. *How did she find out?* He rang the doorbell repeatedly and finally found his keys. As he walked in, he tripped on his suits . . . fell forward and struck his head on the corner of a cardboard carton. "What the hell is this?"

Margaret did not answer. He searched through the house and found her crying beside Matthew's crib. "Take your things."

"What's wrong?"

"Go to her. I can't live like this."

"I told you it's finished."

"I can't stand the sight of you."

"Please—give me another chance. Don't do this to me."

"You're not sharing my bed! Your promises are worthless. I loved you and was rewarded with lies."

Phil sensed his crying act wouldn't change her mind. He preferred she lash out, beat on him and lose self-control. Subconsciously, he needed punishment for being a bad boy, and then he could expect forgiveness. Her determination unnerved him. Before leaving, he called to the nursery, "Please give me another chance. Let me stay."

Margaret screamed, "Get out!"

Chapter 11

At his next session with Doctor Reid, Phil described his despair when Margaret forced him to leave.

"I didn't want to, but she insisted. I'm devastated without her."

"Did you forget the book, on purpose? Perhaps you wanted to give Margaret an opportunity to discover evidence of your betrayal; you wanted her to initiate legal action for divorce. I explained your self-destructive tendencies."

"Yes—but, I love both. I think it's possible to love two women at the same time in different ways. Each fulfills a need. I feel like I'm two separate persons, my personality changes depending on whether I'm with Margaret or Teresa."

"Now you're suggesting schizophrenia."

"Doctors are compelled to label everything. Aren't they? After Teresa's suicide attempt, I asked Margaret to convert the downstairs den room into an apartment and allow Teresa to live with us. Then I could love both and share myself."

"How did she react?"

"She said I'm crazy to think she could live in a polygamous arrangement. I tried to explain my love for both, but I don't understand it myself. She refused to listen."

"Are you relieved that Margaret made the final decision?"

"In a way, yes, although I didn't want to leave her and Matthew. I felt overpowered by the demands on me—torn in two directions. My life is impossible keeping each woman in a separate niche."

"I lied to Margaret; I told her our appointments were every week, instead of once a month. I wrote checks to 'Cash' with your name in the memo portion, and then spent the money on Teresa on the evenings of my fictitious therapy. She made me feel better than you did."

"Theoretically, living with both would end your deceit; you could be totally honest."

"That would solve my problems. I can't know how the women would react."

"Do you expect them to adjust their lives to gratify your selfish needs?"

"Maybe they'll need psychotherapy to cope with me. Then you could tell them it's possible for a man to love two women."

Doctor Reid realized this session had slight effect on Phil's mindset.

"Our time is up and I have another patient waiting. You've given me much to ponder. Have you ever considered a career in psychiatry? I'm never certain whether you're truthful or using me. Since it's your money, let's make another appointment for next week."

"Certainly, Doctor Reid. I feel we made excellent progress tonight."

"It's my job to say whether we made progress."

"I meant . . . . See you next week."

*　　*　　*

Phil picked up the certified letter from his desk with curiosity. The return address, A. Shelby, Esq. Attorney at Law, indicated urgency. Inside, a brief letter requested a meeting to discuss legal separation. Apparently, Margaret would not reconcile.

Phil had moved into Teresa's cramped studio apartment, clearly insufficient for two. Teresa wanted to search for larger quarters immediately. He convinced her to wait until the terms of the agreement are settled.

*　　*　　*

At the attorney's office, Ann Shelby greeted Phil. Her black hair, piercing gray eyes and tall thin figure impressed him as he grasped her outstretched hand.

"Good morning, Mister Noble. I'm Ann Shelby, your wife's advocate. Do you have representation?"

"No. Can we settle this amicably?"

"I advise that you obtain legal counsel. What appears simple on the surface can increase in complexity. If you wish to continue without a lawyer, we will begin when Margaret arrives. Would you care for coffee?"

"No thanks."

Margaret entered and barely glanced at him as Ann continued.

"Now we can start working toward a meaningful solution. Since an infant is involved, it is usual for the mother to nurture the child in its accustomed environment. The child's welfare is imperative."

"I wouldn't have it any other way."

"You realize Mister Noble that your responsibilities include expenses maintaining the household; mortgage, if any, heat and utilities, insurance—also expenses for Margaret's car."

"Yes, I know"

"In addition we'll require child support in the amount of two hundred dollars a week."

"What? How can an infant spend two hundred dollars a week? Outrageous!"

"Have you personally shopped for Matthew's necessities? Children quickly outgrow clothing. Consider yourself fortunate that Margaret refuses support for herself; she intends to resume her career when Matthew is older. Did I mention my fee? Since Mrs. Noble is without resources, you're responsible."

"She wants the separation and I have to pay your legal fee?"

"Those are the facts, Mister Noble—like it or not. If you agree to the terms, I'll prepare the legal documents for both signatures."

Throughout the proceedings, Margaret remained silent. She never considered all the factors presented by Ann Shelby. After seeing Phil's response, she was thankful for Ann's help. *I wish I were home with Matthew, instead of witnessing these legalities. Without Ann, I would struggle to live.*

Phil left the meeting dejected. He never considered his responsibilities. When he explained the terms to Teresa, her face turned livid.

"She gets everything her way. What about us? Aren't we entitled to happiness?"

"In time, my finances will improve. I promise I will earn enough to meet all my obligations—to you as well as Margaret and Matthew. We'll have to put that new apartment on hold for awhile."

"I hate her! If she weren't here, we'd have everything, including Matthew. I wish she were dead!"

"What a horrible thing to say! I know you feel bitter—be patient. We'll work it out."

All week Teresa blamed Margaret for their monetary problems and berated Phil for agreeing to the terms. She begrudged every cent and let Phil know at every opportunity.

*   *   *

After the conditions of separation became effective, Phil experienced a series of ghastly dreams.

In one dream, he found himself on the dark and quiet street in front of the house in Merrick. The glow of the night-light through the nursery window was the only illumination. Margaret and Matthew were asleep. He removed a five-gallon container of gasoline from the trunk of his car and with his key, unlocked the front door—Margaret neglected to call the locksmith. Quickly he doused the fluid throughout the rooms. At the front door, he lit a match and dropped it on the floor. Within seconds, the house became an inferno. Suddenly feeling remorse, he made a futile attempt at a rescue. After the firefighters extinguished the flames, he moaned with grief when they carried out charred remains. He woke from the nightmare shouting, "I didn't mean to do it!" Teresa seized Phil by the shoulders and shook him. "Wake up! Wake up! You were dreaming." Still sobbing, Phil clung to her. "Thank God!" he said, surprising words from a man who never acknowledged God's existence.

In another dream, he and Margaret were alone on a rented sailboat. When they left the dock, a slight breeze, perfect weather for sailing, ruffled the water. Phil prided himself on his seamanship and promised to teach Margaret the basics. They left the bay into the wide expanse of blue ocean water. The swells grew larger as the shoreline receded in the distance, barely visible on the horizon. A sudden squall whipped the canvas sails, the boat lurched, the boom swung from starboard to port. Margaret lost her balance and fell overboard. She screamed, "Help! Help me!" Phil saw the terror on her face as he failed to bring the boat around. Helpless, he watched the orange dot of her life vest and her upright waving arms fade into the distance. He was alone in the silence.

The dreams continued, branded in his mind. Phil built up a hidden anger against Margaret, fueled by Teresa's reluctance to part with any of his income. *Perhaps, if I can charm Margaret into making love to me again, I could break the terms of the separation. The agreement is only a piece of paper; she is still my wife. If I convince her to accept Teresa into our lives, the dreams would stop. Why was she so irrational?* He blamed Margaret for all his problems.

Chapter 12

Three months after their separation, Phil's anger toward Margaret, incited by Teresa's barbs, increased. He missed Margaret's presence in his life—blamed her for the separation—not his infidelity. The conflict between desire and retaliation confused his thinking and bruised his ego. To settle his discomfiture he decided to confront Margaret. A perfect opportunity came when Teresa phoned his office.

"My mother invited me to dinner. Don't worry if I'm late."

After work he drove to Merrick—his thoughts on Margaret. He did not warn her. *A rational person could see how unjustly Margaret treated me. I love her! How can she abandon me? Should I have brought flowers? No—she got enough from me. What excuse can I give for my presence? I'll think of something.* He rang the doorbell.

Margaret opened the door guarded by a chain lock.

"What do you want? You aren't welcome here; go back to Teresa!"

"Please Margaret, I must talk to you."

"We're through talking. Contact my lawyer."

"I came for that wine rack my mother gave us at our housewarming."

"Anything you wanted, you should have taken weeks ago."

The tip of Phil's shoe prevented it from closing.

"It's cold out here. Can't we talk without a chained door between us? I would like to see my son."

"Only for a minute. Matthew is sleeping. Don't wake him."

She followed Phil into the nursery and together they stood alongside the crib. Admiring the sleeping infant, Phil whispered, "He's beautiful." Gently he touched the baby's forehead then the tiny fingers. Margaret observed Phil's tender manner with their child. Phil quietly stepped out of the nursery and walked toward the stairs leading down to the den. Margaret lagged behind him.

When she reached the stairs, Phil was already ascending with the wicker wine rack. He deliberately bumped her with his right shoulder. She fell down the short narrow staircase and landed on the thickly carpeted floor.

Outraged, she attempted to rise. On impulse, he dropped down beside her and tried to kiss her. She struggled; moved her head wildly from side to side while crying.

"Are you crazy? "No! No! Leave me alone!"

In the course of his forced kisses and her fierce struggle, he hesitated for a moment upon tasting blood from her upper lip. His right hand tore her blouse open, while his left hand cupped her bra-covered breast. Insisting on his conjugal rights, he rasped, "You're still my wife, damn it!"

"Phil! You're hurting me. Stop!" Then in a softer voice, she said, "Let me help." Surprised by her compliance, he backed off expecting cooperation; instead, she broke free and dashed out the front door.

Panic-stricken she ran, glancing back. The only sign of life in the neighborhood was the lighted windows of the Bonelli house. Frantic, she pounded on the door.

"Help me! Oh God! Help me."

Mr. Bonelli hardly recognized her—frightened and crying—blouse torn.

"Margaret! What happened? Come in."

"Can I use your phone? My husband lost his mind." Desperate she dialed the police and reported the assault.

Mr. Bonelli gently wiped the blood from her lip with hydrogen peroxide and cotton. Then he gave her ice in a handkerchief to compress the wound, ease the pain and prevent swelling. Flashing lights signaled the arrival of the police car. Accompanied by Mr. Bonelli, she returned home to find Phil calmly explaining to the officer that they merely had a family squabble and apologized for the inconvenience. The police officer saw Margaret. "Did you do that?"

"It was an accident."

"Ma'am, what happened?"

Margaret related the events that led her to report the incident.

"Are you willing to have him arrested?"

Margaret did not want Matthew's father branded a felon with a police record. "No. Warn him to stay away. He doesn't want to accept our separation."

"If this happens again you're going to jail."

"I promise officer. I don't know what possessed me."

The officer turned to Margaret. "If I were you, Ma'am, I'd get an Order of Protection. Do it tomorrow. It may be difficult since you're reluctant to charge him, but a sympathetic judge may act on the basis of your call for help.

"Thank you. I will. Please wait until he leaves." She pointed to Phil.

"How long since the separation?"

Phil answered, "Three months."

"Then everything in the house belongs to her. You should have removed your personal property in the first month."

"Thanks, officer. I won't cause a problem. May I leave now?"

"Since she refuses to charge you with assault and attempted rape, I have no reason to hold you."

Relieved when Phil left with the wine rack, she hurried to the nursery and prayed that her sleeping angel would not inherit his father's dreadful traits.

* * *

In her robe and freshly-scented from her shower; Teresa reclined on the bed reading a Cosmopolitan® article about keeping her man happy in bed—not that she learned anything she hadn't already tried. Phil arrived—smiling. "I'm sorry I'm late."

"What's that?" *Why was he carrying a wine rack? There was hardly room in their cramped apartment for it—the two bottles in the cupboard did not need special storage.*

"I visited Matthew. This wicker wine rack was a house-warming gift from my mother. Margaret insisted I have it."

"I can understand why she wanted to get rid of that hideous old thing. I expected you home by nine and it's after ten. How's Matthew?"

"He's growing daily. I missed him."

Phil acted the devoted parent. *Infants cry, fret, and burp sour milk. I like them older, like little people that I can talk to and relate to. What can you do with a baby?*

"Don't feel sad. Someday, when we have our own home, we'll start our family. After your shower, we'll practice tonight." Her expectation of sex intrigued him, as did her loosely overlapping robe. *Thank God, Margaret did not have me arrested. I could have spent the night in a cold jail cell instead of a warm bed.*

After he dried himself, he approached the bed with the towel loosely tied around his waist. Releasing the towel and pushing the magazine aside, he settled in beside her. He kissed the arc of her neck and earlobes . . . .

* * *

In the morning, Margaret phoned Ann Shelby and related the events leading to the attempted rape. Ann explained that an Order of Protection would prevent Phil's visits completely.

"You were lucky this time. In the future always have another person present during his visits."

Upon Ann's advice, a locksmith installed a dead-bolt lock on the inside of the bedroom door. Since the bedroom was adjacent to the nursery and the connecting wall consisted of two closets, each opening into one of the rooms, she devised a plan of escape. After emptying the closets, she broke through the common wall with a hammer and crowbar. Margaret did the work herself to keep her escape route secret. If an intruder attempted to break into her bedroom, she could slip through the closets into the nursery, grab Matthew and escape through the front door. She feared for herself and Matthew.

That evening she wrote a letter to Ann Shelby stating:

> In the event of my accidental death, I request a complete investigation into the circumstances. I fear for my life since the separation. My husband has attacked me physically and tortured me with tales of recurring dreams, which end in my death by various means. When our divorce is final, I shall be in danger. If he gets custody of Matthew, he gains control of my assets. In my will I bequeath all my property and possessions in trust for my son, Matthew and administered by my parents. Since our home is jointly owned, at least until a final divorce decree, my death would solve his problems; he would be free to live in my house with Teresa and they could raise my son as their own—a thought I hate to consider. God help me.
>
> Margaret Noble

* * *

Her nerves frayed, Margaret jumped at the sound of the doorbell. A florist's deliveryman held a package. She wrote down the name and phone number painted on the side of the truck before opening the door. The man handed her a long white box decorated with red ribbon. She carried the box to the kitchen table. Suspicious after having read newspaper articles about package bombs set to explode when opened, she thought, *this could be one!* She dialed Directory Assistance for the number of the Regal Florist in Merrick to verify the number painted on the truck. Still cautious, she removed the ribbon and slowly opened the box. There were a dozen long-stemmed red roses with a note

> Dearest Margaret,
> I'm sincerely sorry. Please forgive me. My love for you is impossible to deny.
>
> Your husband,
> Phil.

Margaret felt a momentary weakness, until she perceived this gift as one of Phil's ploys. Throwing the note in the garbage, she carefully wrapped the box of roses and enclosed a note to Mrs. Bonelli.

> Dear Elvira,
>   These are for the kindness you have shown me in my time of need.
>
>   Margaret

Chapter 13

Margaret, paranoid with memories of Phil's attack and tales of his dreams describing her death, lived on edge—suspicious of everything. Matthew occupied a major portion of her day and caring for him helped ease her fears. She decided against an Order of Protection that might intensify Phil's violent tendencies. However, she took seriously Ann's warning to have another person present whenever Phil visited. A friend recommended Jenny; a capable, trustworthy, religious Jamaican woman experienced in raising her two children. On Monday and Thursday, Margaret anticipated Jenny's arrival; her ready smile, and lilting voice brought welcome company.

*   *   *

Phil's betrayal upset her equilibrium between love and hate. His presence made the house a home. Even though he worked long hours, she knew that at night they'd share the warmth and comfort of their bed. Her loneliness increased after she tucked Matthew in his crib and she faced the unbearable silence. During Phil's presence, she prepared for bed with a ritual that involved facial cleansers and night creams; she took special care to make herself appealing with sensual fragrances and lacey nightwear. Alone now, she slept in pajamas while wrapping her arms and legs around a body pillow. Matthew alleviated her utter loneliness.

She recalled the difficulty conceiving Matthew. During four years of marriage, they practiced birth control. When they wanted to start a family, nothing happened. At the time her gynecologist did fertility tests, Margaret and Phil, deeply in love, had frequent sex. The doctor found no deterrent to conception, except for bad timing. She became a slave to the thermometer. She would phone Phil's office. "Phil? Come home. It's time!"

How did I come to fear the one person to whom I surrendered body and soul? He was my first love; we were good together.

Phil won her with his boyish charm and adventurous spirit. On the afternoon of their wedding rehearsal at Saint Ann's Church, they arrived to find the door locked. Everyone in the wedding party was present so Phil obtained the key for the church at the rectory. As he unlocked the door, a gray-haired couple approached him and asked, "Father, will you hear our confession?"

"I'm afraid you're mistaken, I'm not a father—yet. We're getting married tomorrow."

"We saw you unlock the church and assumed . . . ."

The flustered woman pulled him away by the arm before he could say more. After Phil related the incident to the others, they called him Father Phil.

Margaret saved her virginity for the wedding night, not by choice but fear of parental disapproval. A religious person, she firmly believed in the teachings of the Catholic Church. During childhood, she imitated the nuns teaching a class of imaginary students. She used a white scarf for a veil—clapped her hands for their attention and scolded them appropriately. Phil proved the ultimate challenge. During their courtship, he teased her constantly, attempting to overcome her inhibitions. She resisted, at times reluctantly; she truly desired him. She prayed to the Blessed Virgin Mother Mary for strength to resist his entreaties. On their wedding day, she stood before the altar having earned the right to wear white. After the long denial, both were eager for the wedding reception to end so they could blend together as one. Their wedding night surpassed all her expectations.

How can I fear this man who loved me—telling me gruesome details of his nightmares? She could not believe when he physically abused her, but the mental abuse was worse—having her life threatened by the person she loved. *What brought our marriage to this horrible state? Phil drifted away after I became pregnant.* He professed whole-hearted support during the pregnancy but worked long hours after Teresa entered his life. Margaret couldn't understand the fascination this other woman held for him. *If I hadn't become pregnant would Phil have left? He had difficulty accepting me as a mother and a wife. Maybe he was jealous of the love and attention the baby demanded. I gave him every chance, forgave him repeatedly, and listened to his false promises only to discover that he was still involved with Teresa. Now, I lost him forever. I can't share him with Teresa, as he wanted; I need his love exclusively. I can't settle for less. Whatever caused the split; the state of my life is forever changed.*

*   *   *

She cherished the good times of their marriage and the joy Matthew gave her, but she was restless. Constant baby talk to Matthew impaired her ability for adult conversation. She needed interaction with people; she needed to feel alive again. Before going on maternity leave, Margaret worked for Ted Burns, the Vice President of Marketing for a national insurance firm. Summoning her courage, she phoned him and requested a meeting. He was pleased to hear from her.

"Come in Monday morning. I'm glad you decided to return."

On Monday, after she left Matthew at mother's house, she drove to Garden City. The morning sun reflected golden beams from the glass exterior of the tall office building. The well-groomed parking lot was almost full. Invigorated, she stepped out of the car, adjusted her skirt and jacket, and walked briskly toward the entrance.

A young slender oriental woman with a dazzling smile occupied the desk outside of Mr. Burns' office.

"Good morning. I'm Margaret Noble."

"Mr. Burns is expecting you. I am Carol. I've been working for Mr. Burns since you left. Would you care for a cup of tea . . . coffee?"

"No thank you, Carol"

Margaret liked her immediately. Yet she felt like an outsider before this girl who could influence her future. Carol spoke to Mr. Burns on the intercom.

"He'll see you now."

Margaret tried to hide her anxiety. Mr. Burns, a tall gracious man with tinges of gray hair at the temples, welcomed her. His voice resonated confidence.

"Good morning, Margaret. You look better than ever. I see motherhood agrees with you. How's the baby? A boy, if I recall."

"Matthew is doing fine."

"I hoped you would call. Would you like coffee?"

"Tea, please—decaf."

Apparently, this would be a lengthy interview; else, he would not have suggested refreshments.

"Margaret, speaking for the firm and myself, we're pleased you decided to join us. We are selecting candidates for an important public relations position. After you indicated interest, I proposed your name to my colleagues and we decided that your prior experience is invaluable. The job is yours, if you want it."

"What does the position entail?"

"We need you to enhance our public image. You would start at an annual salary of fifty thousand dollars including stock options, health benefits, a four-week vacation and eleven paid holidays. After six months, the board will review your performance and may adjust your compensation. Opportunity is unlimited."

This was more than she ever dreamed; she never expected it would be easy.

"You will have a free hand . . . do whatever is necessary to get results. We allocated a budget for the project and you shall have complete control. Refer anyone that questions your authority to me. Now, I'll show you to your office and introduce you to your assistant. Maybe I'm going too fast. Do you accept the job?"

"Yes, I do. I promise I'll do my best."

"I have complete confidence in your ability."

While the stares of coworkers followed them, he led her through the complex to an area free from the normal office bustle. They approached a young man typing on an IBM Selectric™.

"Henry, this is Margaret Noble, your boss. Help her get settled."

Henry glanced up at Margaret and saw a tall trim figure dressed in excellent taste. He expected a male boss.

"We'll make a good team."

She approved his straightforward manner; his direct eye contact while he spoke. In his twenties, he appeared, ambitious and a neat dresser. An immediate attraction, bound them.

"I'm certain we shall, Henry."

Mister Burns led her into a glass-lined office overlooking the landscaped garden and lawn area.

"This is your office. I left a transcript of the Board's last meeting that defines the goals of our company. I also spelled out your job description and authorization codes. Now, I'll leave you to settle in."

"Thank you for the opportunity, Mister Burns."

"Please call me Ted. You're an executive now—get to work!"

Margaret could not believe her good fortune; she returned to an executive position instead of her previous job. She knew former associates envied her sudden rise in the company and depended on Henry's loyalty and friendship to guide her through minefields of jealousy.

Unknown to her, she returned at a time when the company needed a woman executive in management. Publicity in the daily newspapers decried the existence of a 'glass ceiling'. Until now, men held all positions of authority. The Board of Directors voted to create a job in public relations to dispel traces of prejudice regarding the advancement of women within their company, especially women with children. Ted Burns guaranteed the management that Margaret possessed the qualities of intelligence, poise and self-confidence that the firm needs.

Whatever their reasons, Margaret basked in her good fortune. She sat in her plush leather chair behind her rosewood desk and watched the sign painter apply the gold letters of her name and title on the office door—proof that she wasn't dreaming. She opened the drawer on the right side of the desk and found an attaché case covered in cordovan leather with her initials embossed in gold letters.

Margaret, elated, phoned her mother. "I got the job. Not only that, but I got a promotion. So much has happened this morning, I can't believe it. How's Matthew? Does he miss me?"

"Congratulations! He's a happy child—don't worry. We're doing fine. He's busy with his toys now. We'll see you at dinner."

"Thanks Mom. I love you."

Aware of the company's high expectations, she nervously studied the job description. She asked God for guidance.

Chapter 14

Phil returned from Matthew's first birthday party in a joyful mood until Teresa, irritated at being alone in the apartment on a sunny afternoon that she would rather have spent walking in the park or on the beach, asked in a sarcastic tone, "Did you enjoy yourself?"

"Surprisingly, I did. A clown amused the children with stories and formed balloons into hats and animal shapes. His red and yellow costume and ridiculous ball of a nose over his expanded mouth and red wig fascinated Matthew."

"And I suppose you paid for that."

"Teresa, it is his first birthday!"

"How many birthdays will pass before you file for divorce, so we can start our family?"

"Have patience. It takes time."

"Not if you love me."

"All right! I'll make an appointment with the lawyer Monday. I promise."

He understood Teresa's impatience but wanted Margaret to initiate divorce proceedings with the possibility of a settlement in his favor. Financially pressured by support payments, Phil resented Teresa's nagging. His failure to file for divorce clouded their sex life. He couldn't blame Teresa for wanting it all.

*   *   *

Saturday morning, Margaret anticipated spending the entire day with Matthew. Other days she raced against time to bundle him up in his sleep for the ride to his grandmother's house. Today she played, bathed and dressed him at her leisure. She marveled at the warmth and tenderness of his velvety skin as she dried his tiny bottom with gardenia scented baby powder. He kicked her hand away and squirmed to escape her attempts to restrict his freedom; he squealed while she coaxed and laughed at his futile resistance. After putting the nursery in order, she placed Matthew in the playpen, and then poured her mid-morning coffee. Matthew toddled around the perimeter of the playpen and amused himself by throwing toys, to the floor, and insisting his mother pick them up. Ignoring his demands, she picked up the thin Saturday edition of NEWSDAY® and skimmed over the headlines. While reading Dear Abby®, the sound of the door chimes startled her. Still in a housecoat, with hair disheveled and no makeup, she was embarrassed to open the door. Through the cut glass door panel she discerned a gray-haired man holding a brown manila envelop. He appeared grandfatherly and non-threatening. She opened the door still secured by a chain lock.

"Are you Mrs. Margaret Noble?"

"Yes, I am."

"This is for you."

He glanced at the photograph in his other hand. Stretching the chain lock, she accepted the envelope.

"When I saw your picture, I knew you were a lady. The guy that wants to divorce you must be nuts! You're prettier than in the picture."

Upon the word, **_divorce_**, she dropped the envelope as if it had suddenly burst into flames. The finality of the word momentarily stunned her.

The process-server reached through the crack, picked up the envelope and handed it to her.

"Thank you. I know you're only doing your job. Would you care for a cup of coffee?"

"I've had too much already. You're a kind woman. He must be crazy."

Shaking his head in disbelief, he turned and walked to his car.

With a letter opener, she slit the envelope and removed the contents. The word, SUBPOENA, caught her eye. She immediately phoned her attorney.

"Ann, I received a subpoena to appear in court. Phil's filed for divorce."

"Don't worry. Be happy he is initiating the process. That's in your favor."

"I want to appear before the judge with Matthew in my arms and embarrass Phil. I'll tell everyone how he cheated."

"You will not! In fact, I don't want you there; I'll represent you. Phil's attorney and I will hammer out the terms of the agreement prior to the hearing. If you're present with the baby, the judge will assume you care and think there's a possibility of reconciliation. He could delay the process another six months or longer. You're not thinking of reconciling on his terms, are you?"

"Never!"

"That settles it. Leave the rest to me and don't worry. You'll do fine."

Margaret needed Ann's help. This day that started so beautifully left her emotionally drained. She picked up Matthew from the playpen and kissed him on the cheek.

"It's you and me, kid."

*   *   *

Two months elapsed since the subpoena. Phil waited nervously outside the courtroom expecting Margaret at any moment; he dreaded facing her. After today's proceedings, he would have to marry Teresa. Except for Teresa's insistence, he would have delayed forever. *Why couldn't I love both? Why are women so possessive? I forfeited any chance of reconciliation with Margaret. Perhaps, the divorce will ease my life's complexities.*

Ann Shelby walked toward the courtroom with his attorney. *How can they be friends while representing opposite sides?*

"Good morning, Mr. Noble. Mrs. Noble is unable to attend this morning. However, I shall act in her behalf with full power-of-attorney."

"Is she ill? Is Matthew all right?"

"They are quite well. I'll leave you to discuss the provisions of the decree with your attorney. I think you will find the terms reasonable."

Disappointed at Margaret's absence but relieved of face-to-face confrontation, Phil mulled over his ambivalent feelings. He wanted to say that he is sorry for all that happened; that he still loved her and Matthew but also loved Teresa. *I can't explain my feelings to myself; how could I explain them to Margaret? Since she isn't here, it doesn't matter.*

Ann stood before Honorable Judge Beatrice Peck. "Your honor, my client Mrs. Margaret Noble has authorized me to represent her at this hearing. She will not contest the divorce and seeks an agreement with Mr. Noble. I submit a copy of her requests to the court."

"There is a child involved. Is there adequate provision for support and education of that child?"

"Yes, your honor. Mr. Noble is required to maintain a fifty thousand dollar life insurance policy for the child's college education. My client retains the house and Mr. Noble agrees to provide for its maintenance in addition to two hundred dollars a week child support. Mrs. Noble waives alimony."

"Mr. Noble. Do you willingly agree with the provisions outlined by Miss Shelby?"

"Yes, your honor."

"On what grounds are you requesting a divorce?"

"Irreconcilable differences and deprivation of conjugal rights."

"Your child is only a year old; have you tried marriage counseling?"

"No. Counseling would not change her mind. We've lived apart since the child's birth."

"I'm confused—it is your child, isn't it?"

"Yes, your honor."

"Then what is the problem?"

"I'm in love and living with another."

"You want a divorce because of your infidelity. Is that correct?"

"Yes, your honor."

"You don't deserve her. I hereby grant the divorce."

The entire matter took less than fifteen minutes—an eternity for Phil. While the lawyers completed the paper work, Phil walked out of court a free man, although saddled with life-long obligations. *Maybe, the divorce will end my violent nightmares. I'm sorry I related my dreams to Margaret and caused her fear. What's wrong with me?*

*   *   *

After the court appearance, Phil arranged for the term life insurance policy specified in the agreement at his savings bank. While there, he opened his safe deposit box and listed its contents—stocks, bonds, treasury notes and cash. Fortunately, his name alone was on all the securities allowing him liquidation without Margaret's signature. His accumulated wealth surprised him and his spirits lifted—leaving Teresa's apartment appeared possible.

Chapter 15

Holding the divorce decree, Teresa surrendered to Phil's embrace.

"Oh—Phil. Marry me—right away."

"The ink is still damp on Her Honor's signature."

"I'm so happy!"

"Careful, you'll smudge it! It's hardly legible now."

"Let's get the marriage license today."

"The license bureau is closed. I promise we'll be first in line in the morning. Besides, we need blood tests."

"Darn all these rules and regulations. What difference does it make; we've been intimate for a year . . . like being married."

"I guess some people actually wait for their wedding night."

"Why would any one want to?"

"Today let's celebrate my freedom. I have a feeling you won't allow me to enjoy bachelorhood for long."

"Let's celebrate now."

Teresa deftly unzipped him and through the cotton of his underwear playfully manipulated his privates. He jumped at the unexpected contact.

"Teresa, we're in my office! The cleaning people are coming."

"Lock the door, Silly. You've done it before."

Rendered immobile by her touch, he did not respond quickly enough—she locked the door. Then turning toward him dropped her skirt, revealing black lace panties. Phil's excitement enhanced by the risk of discovery, allowed this impetuous woman her way. She unbuckled his leather belt. As he, kicked his trousers aside he slipped her right hand inside his briefs. With gentle pressure, she pulled him down to the thickly carpeted floor. As he lay prone, she teased his inner thighs with kisses before lowering her body and receiving all he had to give. She wanted his baby—without delay.

*   *   *

The next day, Teresa met Phil during lunch hour in Veidell's lobby. After a quick kiss, they headed to a nearby Medical Lab for blood tests. She was apprehensive. "I can't say I'm looking forward to this."

"You don't have anything in your past to hide? Do you?"

"I'm an alien from another planet. My blood circulates at extremely hot temperatures—enough to melt those little plastic test tubes."

"I thought so. Every time we make love, I've experienced that in-your-body experience."

"But, seriously, I cringe any time a needle is pointed in my direction. And when it pierces my skin, I jump."

"You jump with any penetration."

"I don't like it—the needle, I mean. I wish we didn't need tests."

"The law is the law. You want a legal marriage—don't you?"

"I wouldn't settle for less. I promise I'll be your loving wife forever and ever."

As they walked the two short Manhattan blocks to the lab, Phil held a tight grip on her arm.

". . . in case you try to escape."

". . . never happen!"

*   *   *

They married at City Hall without fanfare and a minimal wedding party; his brother Eric served as best man and Alicia, the maid of honor. Teresa's mother and aunt completed the list of invited guests.

Teresa wore a chic white dress embellished with pearls at the neckline and sleeves. A saucy hat with a hint of bridal veil perched on her head. Her high-heeled white satin pumps added height as she stood next to Phil during the five-minute ceremony.

After Eric photographed them outside City Hall, they entered a waiting white stretch limousine. At the entrance of Central Park, Phil and Teresa posed for more pictures then boarded a white gaily-decorated carriage pulled by an off-white horse. The others celebrated in the limo with champagne from its fully stocked bar. Although they could have walked to The Plaza™, Phil instructed the chauffer to drive the circuitous route to the hotel entrance. The wedding party entered the Palm Room™. Teresa's amazed mother and aunt stared in disbelief at the luxurious setting.

After the meal, the wedding party returned to the limo; Phil ordered the chauffer to drive each person home. After many kisses and congratulations, they left still in a party mood. Amid the stares of passersby, Teresa and Phil entered the hotel and retreated to their room for their wedding night, although it was mid-afternoon.

He carried Teresa over the threshold. Inside their suite, she refused to remove her arms from his neck.

"I'm going to hold you forever."

Wincing from a sharp pain in his back, he dropped her on the bed. She pulled him down with her and they lay resting, fully clothed, with the bright afternoon sunlight streaming in.

"Marriage has already changed us; we've never been in bed together unless we were nude." Phil observed.

Teresa replied, "We can easily fix that."

$$*\quad *\quad *$$

Phil could not help thinking, how different this wedding is from the day he married Margaret; the big church reverberating with beautiful organ music. The kiss after the priest pronounced them husband and wife. At the reception, a six-piece band provided the dance music. The events of today are subdued in comparison.

He recalled Margaret's shyness while standing before him in a silken white robe that discretely revealed her perfect body. He cherished the memory of shared passion . . . the climactic moment long denied him.

The mystery was lacking this afternoon. The intimate knowledge they already shared during long lunch breaks and months of living together dulled the surprise. However, Teresa always managed to arouse his passion; she still possessed that magical power to fascinate him. Would their union be different now, dwelling on procreation rather than sexual gratification? *Will I have the same problem dealing with her pregnancy that I had with Margaret's? What am I thinking? Why, suddenly, does it feel like a duty to have sex with my lovely bride? I would rather have an ongoing relationship with Teresa without marriage; she insists on nothing less than marriage—as she insists on having a baby I hope my actions will not reveal my concerns.*

Teresa appeared with a sensual glow visible through the pleats of her white lace baby doll lingerie. Phil excused himself. "Whatever you're planning, hold the thought while I freshen up."

As he removed his shirt, he detected body odor; he had perspired profusely during the ceremony. A warm shower removed vestiges of his discomfort. He compared his preparation as if he were a sacrificial lamb. After drying, he reached for a white terry-cloth robe. Before touching her, he popped the cork on the chilled champagne and attempted to catch the effervescent liquid. He poured two glasses and proposed a toast. "May we be forever happy in our love."

Phil slowly sipped the champagne, and gazed into her eyes. Shall we . . . , Mrs. Noble?"

He closed the drapes to eliminate the glaring afternoon sun and bathe their room with light pink glow. He lifted her in his arms and seated her on the edge of the bed. Standing before her, he slipped the straps of the baby doll lingerie from her shoulders. With her upper body exposed, she reached inside his robe and then trapped his member within her cleavage. Her innovative behavior dispelled doubts about their marriage; she knew how pleasure him with her body. Suddenly Teresa moved away. *I can't become pregnant through this activity.* They made love until satiated—they slept.

Phil awakened first. He reached over running the tips of his fingers down her smooth belly and thighs, coming to rest on their hairy junction. She stirred to his touch and lazily opened her eyes like a cat ready to purr. Instinctively, she opened herself to him. He wanted to accept, but could not. An invigorating shower might help, but he had not counted on Teresa following him. While washing his hair and face, other hands soaped his body. Before long, she coaxed him into a repeat performance.

*   *   *

Married on Friday, they planned the weekend at The Plaza™ for a mini-honeymoon. The next day, they awakened late. Phil asked, "What shall we do today?"

"With all these fabulous stores along Fifth Avenue, I thought we might go shopping."

"Did you have any special place in mind?"

"I always wanted to shop at Tiffany™."

Phil winced from an imaginary pain in his wallet. *I have to indulge her.*

"To browse, I hope."

"Naturally. I know we can't afford anything expensive; we're saving for a house. However, it would be fun to pretend I'm a millionaire."

"I would give you the world if I could."

Like a couple of flighty tourists they enjoyed the sounds, sights and scents of the city. They observed its inhabitants, explored the wooded pathways in Central Park where squirrels scampered through the grass and pigeons shared lunches. The city had much to offer. On Monday morning, weary and happy, they checked out of the luxurious Plaza™ and returned by limo to their humble Kew Gardens apartment.

Chapter 16

The court awarded Margaret joint custody with the provision that Phil visit Matthew on alternate weekends from noon Friday until 3:00pm Sunday, and for a one-month vacation every year and alternate holidays. Judge Peck wanted Matthew's childhood to include a father's influence.

In preparation for Matthew's first visit, Teresa went on a frenzied shopping spree for all the necessities: baby food, soaps, shampoos, oil, powder and Pampers®. She bought a folding playpen with soft padding for Matthew to play and sleep in. If Matthew were an infant instead of a toddler, she would have equipped a nursery. *I'll pretend he is my child; I'll show Phil that I'm a good mother.*

* * *

Teresa rang the bell. Margaret, with Matthew in her arms, opened the door. Teresa reached for him, but Margaret deliberately ignored her and handed the child to Phil.

"I packed his favorite toys and blanket. He will not sleep without them. Please, take good care of my little baby."

Teresa seeking acknowledgement as Phil's wife answered, "I will."

"I wasn't speaking to you! Phil, will you please watch him at all times. Phone me if you have any questions or problems."

"Don't worry. I love him too. Wave 'bye to Mommy."

"'Bye Matthew, Mommy loves you." Tears welled in Margaret's eyes when she surrendered Matthew. Not to upset Matthew, Margaret forced a smile.

At curbside, Phil adjusted the child seat while Teresa held Matthew and kissed his hands and forehead, aware that Margaret disapproved. Matthew basked in the unexpected attention, and since he loved riding in a car, he was willing to leave his mother.

They tended to Matthew the entire weekend. Teresa suggested they eat at McDonald™, a favorite of mothers with children. In the restaurant Matthew behaved like a normal child of nineteen months. Guided by the example set by his peers he ate bits of chicken—smeared his face with catsup from the French fries—dropped some and pointed to the floor urging retrieval—and finished his Happy Meal® by spilling his drink. Teresa washed his hands and face in the women's restroom. She reveled in the joyful sounds of children playing while the racket irritated Phil.

The play area, designed to appeal to preschoolers, included a plastic slide tunnel and a miniature carousel with its repetitive music. Teresa hovered over Matthew while other mothers, veterans of the McDonald™ scene, let their offspring fend for themselves. Matthew's eyes opened wide with apprehension when Teresa strapped him on a red and white stallion and it moved. This was his first experience on a carousel but observing the children on other mounts dispersed his fear. Before long, he imitated their daring actions, holding the bar and bouncing his bottom on the saddle of his plastic horse urging it to go faster. When Teresa attempted to remove him from the saddle, his piercing screams challenged her patience. Unaccustomed to a child's tantrums, she gently spanked his buttocks and regretted her action immediately, fearful that Phil had seen. They left the restaurant, Matthew crying until the motion of the car lulled him to sleep.

He awoke with the sound of the closing elevator door and the sudden upward jolt. Frightened, Matthew's cries echoed in the confined space. Teresa vainly attempted to calm his fear; she started to doubt her qualifications for motherhood.

After his bath, Teresa changed Matthew into pajamas and placed him in the playpen. At first, he recognized his favorite toy and blanket, but later discovered himself in a strange environment and cried until, exhausted, he slept.

"You've given me responsibility for Matthew; at least help me clean up. We need a larger place."

"I'm doing my best. I have difficulty relating to children his age. When he is older, we'll have more in common and do things together."

"So what am I supposed to do until then? When will we have our own home? When will we have our baby? Why are we waiting?"

Phil's silence aggravated her. With the apartment a shambles, she went to bed, pretending to sleep when he joined her.

*   *   *

Teresa's spirits soared when, at breakfast, Phil announced, "Let's go house-hunting today."

"Are you serious? Don't disappoint me."

"I mean it. Get ready."

She fed and bathed Matthew. She sang inane nursery rhymes while dressing him for their outing. Phil studied the Real Estate section of the New York Times® looking for a home in Merrick on Long Island. Armed with a map and newspaper with ads of prospective houses boldly circled, he drove down Queens Boulevard toward Grand Central Parkway. Teresa was happy and her joy contagious; Matthew behaved in his car seat and Phil sang along with the radio. Another of Teresa's dreams was on the verge of reality.

*   *   *

After three months of house hunting, an eternity to Teresa, she and Phil signed the mortgage and numerous confusing documents, Although she preferred a luxurious home like Margaret's, she settled for a house in Seaford, a sharp contrast to the apartment. She arranged for a two-week vacation to prepare the house for occupancy.

After connecting the utilities, she exulted in the constant parade of artisans and deliverymen. She selected light pastel colors for the walls and supervised the painters to the point that exasperated, they were ready to leave; except the longer, they worked the higher their charges. After the painters completed their work, the interior decorator came with workers to install the window treatments to Teresa's approval. As the furniture arrived, she examined each piece for the slightest flaw before permitting the deliverymen to leave. *Phil will be impressed with my decorating and homemaking abilities.*

During the two happy weeks she worked on the house, they moved personal items, clothing, and the television she bought with Frank's insurance money. Phil commuted by train, while she used the car. After work, he helped at the house, and then drove back to the apartment. The day her vacation ended, they packed the last of their belongings. When she relinquished the keys. Teresa said, "In a way, I'll miss this place. Here I started living on my own. I've had many happy moments here."

*   *   *

Teresa prepared herself for their first night in their new bed. A bubble bath covered her to the chin in luxurious foam as she playfully lifted each leg and swiveled her ankle from side to side like a periscope. Through the open door, Phil, amused by her antics, observed her reflection in the mirror. The last two weeks, he felt neglected—jealous of her preoccupation with the house. While he watched, she raised both ankles out of the water, slipped on the slick bottom and submerged. With hair soaked and a face covered with soap bubbles, she came up sputtering, screaming for a towel. Phil rushed into the bathroom.

"Are you trying to drown yourself?"

She stood up, grasping for the towel that Phil playfully dangled out of reach.

"Phil! Stop that! I can't see! There's soap in my eyes."

Helpless she bent over the washbasin as she rinsed her face and hair. With another towel, he dried the glistening drops from her rounded shoulders and back while he kissed her damp skin. He lifted her to the bed. Phil's spontaneity thwarted her plans, but pleased her tremendously. She had intended to wear lacy lingerie with seductive perfume and use Mama Louise's love potion for added impact.

Chapter 17

When Matthew left for his first visit with his father, Margaret was despondent while she gathered toys from the floor. She missed him terribly; his absence left a disturbing quiet in the house. She went through the mechanical motions of her household tasks. *Will he prefer them to me? What is he doing? Does he miss me?*

To occupy her mind during Matthew's absence, she decided to arrange the clothing in her closet. She chanced upon the dress she wore when she met David at Copperfield's™. Pleased that it still fit her after her pregnancy she recalled how quickly from infancy Matthew and David bonded. Whenever Margaret dressed and applied cosmetics, he anticipated David's arrival followed by trips to the park, the beach and other interesting places. When she dressed him, he called out "David! David!" At home, they played or watched television with him until bedtime. Margaret and David seldom enjoyed a private moment.

Margaret knew David loved her and understood his reluctance to marry—his difficulty accepting the role of instant fatherhood and the responsibility of nurturing another man's child. She needed him to take the initiative, to accept that she and Matthew are a package deal; it's either both or none. She weighed the wisdom of continuing their relationship in its present form. She loved David, but required an indication of marriage in the near future. To arouse David's jealousy, she dated other men. None of these diversions provided the common interests and affection she shared with David.

She kept no secrets and told David that without a commitment and an engagement ring she would continue to date. He didn't like it but never forbade her. Even if he did, she wouldn't have listened. She hoped to shock him from his lethargy by casually mentioning where her date was taking her. Later those same evenings, by strange coincidence, he appeared and made his presence known. If she had devoted herself to him, exclusively their relationship would never progress. She hoped his love would prevail over his parent's objections to a mixed faith marriage.

David arranged a meeting with his parents. He wanted them to know her before making rash judgments. Over tea, they tactfully asked Margaret questions concerning her parents, school and childhood. From her responses, they gathered that she was not Jewish and avoided discussion regarding religion or nationality. Margaret charmed them with her manners, beauty and friendliness, although his mother did not understand why a girl who apparently loved her parents, lived alone. David closely watched their expressions for approval.

One evening, while shopping, his mother's busybody neighbor saw Margaret with David. David was pushing a stroller. The neighbor couldn't wait to report the incident. Immediately upon arriving home, she phoned David's mother. "I saw David and a girl with red hair shopping. Your son was pushing a stroller. Is that her child?"

His mother, although surprised, claimed full knowledge. "Yes, she has a son. David told me about him. He's a little doll, isn't he?" Inwardly she was angry with David for keeping the child secret.

David expected trouble when he arrived home. His mother ignored him and pretended to alter a dress while his father expecting a confrontation, stared fixedly at the television. David sensed the cold welcome and immediately took the offensive. "Don't say a word! Margaret is divorced, a Catholic and has a child—and I'm going to marry her!"

Shocked and helpless, they watched him run up the stairs to his room and decided against a futile encounter. The divorced with a child part, they could handle because David's sister divorced after bearing three children. The inter-faith marriage bothered them more.

David ate breakfast in silence until his mother broached the subject. "Would Margaret raise your children Catholic?"

"We discussed the issue and since this is my first marriage, she agreed that I choose the religion of our children."

"You're already talking marriage. Aren't you rushing things?"

"Don't worry mom. We discussed having children. Any child by me will be of Jewish faith. Margaret and Matthew will remain Catholic."

"It will be difficult to raise children of two faiths in the family. Usually children follow the mother's religion."

"Mom, we've discussed this thoroughly and she promised that she would study and teach our children Jewish traditions, and observe the holy days."

This knowledge eased their reluctance to accept Margaret.

The following evening David and Margaret discussed the engagement with his parents. Margaret calmed their fears.

"We understand your feelings about inter-faith marriage. We love each other and aren't children anymore. We'll work it out."

On subsequent visits, she brought Matthew. His winning ways softened their hearts. Before long, Margaret and David's mothers were discussing the colors of gowns for the wedding.

Chapter 18

When their workday finished, Teresa met Phil at the building entrance and shared a taxi to Penn Station. Adept at outwitting the crowd, they estimated the exact spot on the Long Island Rail Road™ train platform where the doors opened. The first one to enter commandeered a seat for the other by placing a handbag or attaché case on the adjoining seat. Settled in for the ride, Teresa read a novel and Phil dozed—unless new office gossip surfaced. They succumbed to a daily routine along with the same people in the same seats.

Two months passed since they moved into their new home. Teresa was inexplicably restless. She hated the sound of the alarm clock in the morning. She habitually listened to the radio for the weather forecasts; the cheerful voices mingled with music selected to jump-start another day annoyed her as did Phil with his nagging, "Aren't you ready yet? Hurry or we'll miss our train."

Recently she awoke with excessive mood swings, sometimes cheerful, other times grouchy. Phil learned to cope. Then one morning she rushed to the bathroom and vomited. "Go without me. I don't feel well."

". . . you sure you'll be all right?"

"I'll be fine. Last night's seafood salad must have disagreed . . . . I'll rest."

A gross picture of her retching on the train formed in his mind. He hesitated, and then kissed her—on the cheek—guilty for leaving and his lack of compassion.

Teresa's appetite vanished; however, she managed a cup of tea. She knew about morning sickness while pregnant. *Could it be . . . ? Did I conceive on the night I almost drowned in the tub? Phil was extremely passionate. He cannot expect me to work during pregnancy!* She phoned her gynecologist for an appointment.

*   *   *

She planned a special evening to demonstrate her culinary prowess; cook his favorite meal, shrimp scampi and linguine with fresh semolina bread followed by a tiramisu dessert and espresso. *That should impress him!*

In the afternoon, she faced the distasteful task of shelling and cleaning the shrimp. With manicured fingernails, she meticulously peeled the slimy crustaceans, placed the shells in a plastic bag and the meaty part in a dish, occasionally confusing the sort. She covered the dish with plastic wrap and placed it in the refrigerator. After that she rested.

She glanced at the clock. Phil's train, if on schedule would soon arrive. Estimating the cooking time for linguine, she brought a pot of water to a boil. Then she separated four cloves of garlic from the main bulb, peeled the outer layers and sliced the cloves. To remove the strong garlic odor from her fingertips she vigorously scrubbed them with half of a lemon. After immersing the linguine, she waited ten minutes before cooking the shrimp, garlic and olive oil in the frying pan. Two minutes later, her timing perfect, Phil's car sounded in the driveway.

The pungent odor of cooking greeted Phil. To his surprise, it originated in his kitchen and not in the neighbor's . . . . After he checked the day's mail in the hall, he entered the dining room and found the table set with a linen tablecloth, a floral centerpiece, two candles and their finest china.

Standing behind her, he placed his arms around her waist, kissed the side of her neck. "What's the occasion?"

"No occasion. You work hard and I want to please you. Dinner is ready in a minute. Make yourself useful; light the candles."

"I want to know—why the royal treatment?"

"I'm afraid that I've been moody lately."

"How could I miss?"

"I have an appointment with my gynecologist—I have a feeling."

"Do you really think you're . . . ?"

Phil rose from his chair and hugged her. *"How can a woman find happiness in the inevitable pain of childbirth?*

*   *   *

Teresa drove Phil to the train; she needed the car to shop for baby and maternity clothes. She quickly adapted to the role of devoted homemaker and mother and took full advantage of her condition with a leave of absence from work. She knew Phil would indulge every whim.

Phil welcomed commuting alone if only to avoid constant talk about the baby, expected the middle of November. Phil started work earlier and stayed later to complete a vital project. With the added responsibility and Theresa's flagrant spending, he needed the money. In the fourth month of Teresa's pregnancy,

Phil successfully completed his project. A promotion with a substantial salary increase followed; their income sufficed without depending upon her working.

She recalled the poverty that followed the death of her father—the hardship to survive and feed his family. Except for her brother, she had no surviving males in the family. If the pattern follows, she might be in the same predicament. One evening she approached Phil. "I've been thinking about something everyone tends to delay. I want to provide for our baby's future. Life insurance is a good investment and the premiums are less at our age. With payroll deductions we could manage. The baby has given me a new perspective on life. I never want him or her to know the poverty I suffered."

"I'll think about it. I'll talk to my agent tomorrow."

The following day Phil phoned his agent and purchased pending a health examination by the company's physician, a life insurance policy for one million dollars, naming Teresa beneficiary. Once the child is born, he would add its name. When he informed Teresa, she praised his concern for their welfare and security.

*   *   *

One night, he had a dream. He drove to Merrick to visit Matthew and when he arrived he saw the window curtain move. On previous visits Margaret didn't appreciate his presence in her house; he waited curbside for Matthew. Margaret appeared in the doorway in a long white robe, and then walked to the car. Her silken voice stirred dormant memories of their marriage. "Matthew isn't ready. He's sleeping and if I awaken him, he can be quite unmanageable. Would you like to wait inside? I have coffee on."

As she leaned on the edge of the car window, a slight breeze opened the top of her robe offering a glimpse of curving breast. Phil eagerly accepted the invitation and followed her inside. She pointed to a chair at the kitchen table and set a coffee mug on the place mat. While she poured, the scent of her body overpowered the coffee fragrance. The curve of her trim non-pregnant body encased by the clinging robe enticed him.

Still in the dream, he followed her upstairs to the nursery to sleeping Matthew and his teddy bear. Phil said, "He's getting big."

". . . and mischievous." Margaret added.

Not wishing to disturb the child both backed out of the room. At the door, Phil stopped momentarily and Margaret collided with him. His arms encircled her, while he gently guided her into the master bedroom. Their lips met. He lowered her to the bed and her tense body relaxed in ultimate surrender. At the climactic moment, his body shuddered and he awoke—his eyes opened wide. A faint odor reached his nostrils. He touched his sticky groin. *I cheated on my wife in a wet dream—while she lay beside me in our bed!*

Without waking Teresa, he quietly left the bed and carefully closed the bathroom door. With the faucet on low, he washed all trace of ejaculate from his body and then rinsed evidence of his dream from his pajama bottoms before dropping them down the clothes chute.

*　　*　　*

By her fifth month, Teresa gained considerable weight and her short stature accented her protruding belly. Phil found intercourse uncomfortable with that hard little mound pressed against him. In contrast, Margaret's lean figure increased his libido. Sex with Teresa ceased. As her pregnancy progressed, Phil became restless. Prior to marriage, they discussed the concept of an open marriage—if they wished, each could date others and wearing wedding rings was not required. Phil believed a person could love more than one person at the same time. The longer he avoided intercourse with Teresa the more this concept appealed to him. The weird dry run while he dreamt changed his behavior. With ease, he absolved himself of guilt because his infidelity was merely the product of his subconscious. It was a small step for him to justify cheating, maybe not with Margaret, but with any opportune woman.

*　　*　　*

Waiting at the Charlotte, North Carolina airport arrivals terminal, Ms. Beverly Douthart, Interior Decorating Consultant, watched the airport monitor for American Airlines™ flight 635 arrival at gate 22. Her job required that she escort buyers to numerous furniture showrooms and assist ordering and coordinating their selections. Phil's visit entailed purchasing furniture to renovate three executive offices. She could earn a sizable commission.

Her eyes alternated between Phil's photograph in the Veidell organization pamphlet and the arriving passengers. She scanned their faces for a match. In the photo, Phil wore a business suit, white shirt and gray tie. If he traveled in casual clothing, she feared she might miss him. A tall dark-haired man, carrying an attaché case and dressed in a colorful sports shirt and khaki pants fit the description. She couldn't mistake his angular chin, heavy dark brows and steel-gray eyes. She approached him. "Mister Noble?"

"Yes. And you are . . . ?"

"Beverly Douthart, but please call me Bev. Since we'll be working together today, there's no need for formality."

"I agree, Bev. Please call me Phil."

"We'll visit many furniture showrooms. I'll help with your selections and arrange the best deals."

"Perhaps we can discuss our itinerary over breakfast? Where do you recommend we eat?"

"There's a diner near our first stop. Do you have luggage?"

"No . . . lead the way."

She guided him through the terminal to her mobile office, a customized van.

They reviewed their plans over breakfast. Beverley bore a remarkable resemblance to Margaret; except that Beverly's blonde hair flowed over her shoulders. Her slate-blue eyes were the color of her silk blouse. Worn jeans and gray walking shoes completed her outfit. Hanging dark blue plastic earrings, although simple, accented her angular chin and full lips. Traces of freckles sprinkled her fair complexion.

She outlined their itinerary between sips of tea, while Phil ate breakfast and listened attentively with an occasional nod of agreement. He delighted in the sound of her melodious drawl, and the movement of her pink lips. Reluctant to end this pleasurable conversation, he motioned for the check.

By two in the afternoon, they visited three showrooms. This indefatigable woman walked him through miles of furniture displays. The pain in his leg muscles drew attention to his lack of an exercise regimen. *If Teresa saw me in the company of an attractive single woman, she would prohibit all business trips.*

On the way to the next showroom, Phil saw a clean inviting restaurant and suggested they break for lunch. Upon entering both headed for the restrooms. Phil took an inordinate amount of time to clean his fingernails and comb his hair. He returned to Beverly, already seated at a table while the waitress effortlessly recited the day's specials. After ordering, Phil studied Beverly's face as they reviewed their list of purchases and crossed out completed items.

They shared many traits—ambition, determination, eloquence and independence—even the color of their eyes, except hers was a softer gray. His affinity toward her resembled that of a twin; she anticipated his thoughts before he spoke. An hour passed in animated conversation and they had two more showrooms to visit. Beverly suggested they leave. The pleasure of her company during luncheon made him reluctant to resume business. At day's end, the orders placed, they relaxed. Beverly, pleased with her commission, beamed. Phil said "Thank you for a successful day. Would you consider dinner at my hotel? I hate eating alone."

"I'd love to . . . but I'd like to freshen up after our busy day."

"You can use my room. I'll wait in the lounge."

". . . sounds good to me."

At the hotel, Phil gave her his key and proceeded to the bar for a martini. A baseball game was in progress on the television. Since Phil was not a sports advocate, his mind wandered toward the fascinating woman in his room. *What's she doing now?* Sipping the martini, Phil welcomed its soothing effect. He fought a losing battle with thoughts of Beverly. Temptation overcame his good sense and he seized the opportunity. At the registration desk, he told the clerk that he locked his key in the room. After he provided identification, she gave him a spare key. Quietly he unlocked the door and opened it a crack, then entered. Seated on the bed, he heard the shower splashing and visions of Beverly's sleek wet body flashed through his mind. He listened lost in fantasy, until Beverly, wrapped in a towel, walked in. "What are you doing here?"

"I thought you might need help."

"Well, I don't, so you can leave—now! Sex is not a part of our consulting agreement. Please—leave!"

Phil assumed she was attracted to him and attempted to embrace her. Her resistance surprised him. The towel fell as she broke loose and ran toward the bathroom.

"I'm leaving. I misunderstood. Forgive me. Meet me in the lounge as we planned. Permit me to make amends."

"I'll meet you at the bar, if you promise to behave like a gentleman."

Prior to Beverly's rejection, he considered himself irresistible. Phil regretted his impulsive behavior only because it failed. When Beverly approached him at the bar, he found her attractive and charming. "I'm disappointed you thought I was easy. My private life is my own and separate from business. Can we remain friends?"

"I sincerely apologize."

"Apology accepted. I'm famished."

Phil slept restless and alone that night, haunted by the memory of Beverly running from him. In the morning, he checked out of the hotel and boarded a courtesy van to the airport. Unable to sleep during the bumpy flight from Charlotte to La Guardia, he attributed the dull ache in his groin to his frustrating experience with Beverly. His desire and the expectation of a casual conquest recalled the tortures of puberty. Then, he relieved the pressure manually, but after his first experience with a woman, he conserved his energy.

Although he needed Teresa, he experienced difficulty overcoming his aversion to her pregnancy. The vision of her supple velvet body before the baby haunted him. *If only I could see her that way again.* Finding solace in work, he decided to go to the office.

The first passenger to disembark, Phil reached for an available phone and dialed. "Hi Teres'."

"Phil! Where are you? What time will you be home?"

"I have to stop by the office."

"I miss you. Can't you take the rest of the day off?"

". . . with all the work that piled up during my absence?"

"It's not your fault."

"After I finish, I promise to devote the entire weekend to you. I couldn't sleep. Damn! I missed you so." Phil felt a twinge of guilt; erotic thoughts of Beverly caused his sleepless night. "Last night was our first night apart since we married. Lying alone in bed, I missed you. I'll be home as soon as I can."

"Don't be late. I missed you too."

Phil entered a waiting cab to take him to Manhattan.

* * *

An accumulation of notes, including one from Beverly, awaited his return. Although he savored her delicious drawl, he decided to call later and enjoy her voice at his leisure. An urgent note from Mister Veidell demanded his presence and all department heads at 4:00pm. Phil dreaded telling Teresa about the meeting on his first day home after an over-night trip. Teresa answered the phone. "Hello?"

"Hi Teres'"

"Phil—are you leaving?"

"Mister Veidell called a staff meeting. I'll probably be late."

"I knew it! I planned a special evening."

"I'm sorry I didn't come directly home from the airport. I'll phone you the minute the meeting ends. 'Bye—I love you."

Phil listened to an eloquent silence before the click that severed the call.

He took Beverly's business card from his pocket and dialed. *No sense having everyone angry at me.*

* * *

A meeting of the department heads with the Chief Executive Officer presiding signaled bad news. Managers searched their memories for clues to the culprit responsible for this meeting. The firms stock was stable. Sales had slackened as it usually did during a hot summer, but otherwise business appeared normal.

After the assemblage had time to squirm and fear the unexpected, the CEO, Brad Veidell entered the conference room and strode briskly to the chair at the head of the long oak table. "The direction of our company made this meeting necessary." His expression displayed displeasure at the status quo, and then suddenly changed into a benevolent, kinder look. "I want to help. Starting with the person at my right, tell me of any problems within your department that hinder reaching our common goal. Do you have interdepartmental problems . . . any problems with our suppliers?"

Phil thought *the old man is shrewd. He is gathering ammunition to use later against the very people asking for assistance. Moreover, these suckers are falling for his ploy.* So when Mister Veidell asked, "How about you, Noble?" Phil replied, "Everything's going exceptionally well."

"Surely there must be some way I can help; to expedite the work of our sub-contractors or shipments from our suppliers." Then he launched his favorite grenade—"Are you getting cooperation from other departments?" Brad Veidell struggled to conceal his impatience.

"My projects are on schedule." Phil insisted, trying to maintain a serious facial expression. *The others are digging their own graves with the information they volunteered.*

"I called you together to brainstorm a way out of our current loss of revenue. Sales have diminished considerably which resulted in a proportionate drop in the bottom line."

Phil surmised Mr. Veidell intended to stir up all departments and intimidate his employees. Veidell continued his harangue mercilessly and if anyone dared look at the clock or wristwatch, he added another ten minutes. Phil thought he was in the clear until Veidell pointed a finger at him and with a tinge of sarcasm said, "All of you have problems, except Phil. You will continue to have problems unless we cut our expenses. We can't spend as usual and expect sagging profits to support our lifestyles. Something has to give."

I hope he doesn't expect me to cancel my orders with Beverly. If he does, she could perceive the cancellation as a vindictive act for her refusal. Worse, suppose he cuts our salaries. With the baby due in August, we would be financially strapped. Could he be on a 'fishing' expedition, with the prospect of dismissing anyone? Phil provided no information and that exasperated Mr. Veidell. Phil was tempted to look at his watch, but didn't dare. *Teresa must be fuming.*

The meeting lasted two and a half hours before Mister Veidell released his captive audience. At his desk, Phil tried Beverly's number—no answer. Then he called Teresa. "With luck, I may be home before nine o'clock."

"Don't rush on my account. When you get here, you'll get here."

"Teres', please don't be angry. I couldn't help it. I'm sorry."

Teresa lie awake, disappointed that Phil hadn't come home immediately after arriving at La Guardia. Inside, her anger smoldered—ready to flare up at the first word of his well-prepared apology. *It isn't going to work—this time.*

The key turned in the lock, the door opened, his footsteps sounded on the marble floor. She pictured him searching for her in the dark house, illuminated only by the night light outside their bedroom. He raced up the stairs, two steps at a time, until he reached the bedroom door . . . he sighed with relief when he saw her. She feigned sleep while Phil showered and prepared for bed. When he slid alongside her, she moved and turned her back toward him but said nothing, hoping to confuse him by her restrained behavior. Her flesh tingled with the coolness of his skin when he turned toward her and held her close—like two spoons—his arm over her bulging waist. She felt his lips on her neck and with difficulty ignored them. She arched her back with the pleasure of his touch. His arousal rubbed against her sensitive area—a feeling she missed for months. *He must have missed me!* Of its own volition, her body assumed a fetal position, knees drawn up and slightly parted allowing him easy access. She delighted having him inside her . . . the slight gentle movements. Her anger ebbed as she pressed against him.

This wordless lovemaking, minus discomfort to her pregnant body, revealed an unexpected gentleness. When she felt his love within her, her tensions vanished. *How fortunate that I didn't greet him at the front door and vent my anger at his neglect.* She moved away—turned her body—caressed his face and whispered, "Welcome home, darling."

Chapter 19

The sterile walls of the delivery room echoed with Teresa's cries as she panted, huffed and screamed in response to the contractions. At her side, Phil's encouraging "You can do it." didn't help her excruciating pain. She thought childbirth would be a joyous experience. If she didn't believe in that fraudulent premise—had known the pain involved—she might never have married. Now, she doubted the security and comfort Phil provided, was worth this extreme torture.

The attending obstetrician bore little resemblance to the woman she had seen during office visits. A little green cloth cap covered her long blond hair; a white gauze surgical mask hid her pleasant smile. A green hospital jacket and pants covered the rest of her. Paper booties protected her shoes. The only clue to her gender was her feminine voice, instructing Teresa when to breath and push. Teresa chose a woman obstetrician for understanding and compassion; at this moment, she didn't care who caught the baby as long as she regained control of her body.

The pain, the involuntary contractions, each increasing in severity, never-ending, ripped through her body. Her cries drowned out the doctor's voice. *I'm going to die!* She let out a deafening scream—the pressure eased—the infant welcomed the world with cries of protest.

The doctor held the howling baby for her to see, umbilical cord still attached. "You have a boy!"

After cutting the umbilical cord, she passed the baby on to a waiting nurse to aspirate, clean, place an identification band, make an imprint of the baby's foot and record the length and weight. Phil fought a queasy stomach and averted his eyes from his newborn son. *Some husbands regard attending the birth of their child one of life's greatest experiences. Not me! I'd rather pace in the waiting room and have the doctor inform me when all is over.*

In her hospital room a transporter and a nurse's aide lifted her from the gurney to the bed and adjusted it for her comfort. Exhausted and still groggy, Teresa asked, "Phil, have you seen the baby?"

"He's beautiful."

"I never want to go through that again."

"Teres'—people have children. It's a natural process."

"Now that I've given you a son, I've done my share."

"Wouldn't you like a little girl?"

"I'll never go through childbirth again. Maybe I'm selfish, but that's how I feel."

"Suppose—in time—you'll forget the pain and decide you want a girl?"

"We'll adopt. The best gift you could give me is to have a vasectomy. Why should contraception always be a woman's problem?"

"I think this is the wrong time for discussion. If it will make you happy, I'll agree to the vasectomy—when I'm ready."

*   *   *

Mathew, awed by the squirming infant in the crib, was confused and pleased. He heard his father say, "This is your brother. His name is Daniel but you may call him Danny."

Phil holding a camera, placed Danny on the sofa with Matthew seated alongside. Fascinated with this new toy, Matthew attempted to touch the baby's eyes. Teresa quickly pushed his hand aside and scolded, "Don't ever do that! You'll hurt the baby!"

The flash occurred as Matthew broke into tears. Losing interest in Danny, Matthew returned to play with familiar toys that did not get him in trouble. He sensed that Teresa favored the baby and experienced his first feeling of jealousy—he wanted to go home to his mother.

Phil felt a greater bond with Matthew after Danny's birth. Now that Matthew was older, they did things beyond the capacities of an infant. At the park, Phil pushed Matthew high on the swings, until the boy shrieked with delight. Phil taught him to catch a large plastic red and blue ball, and then throw it back; whenever Matthew threw the ball, his eyes looked at Phil but the ball would veer off-target, occasionally landing in someone's picnic lunch. They ended their walk with vanilla ice cream cones. Matthew inevitably fed an entire ant colony when his treat ended on the sidewalk. Phil would then give his cone to Matthew. Phil enjoyed and anticipated their time together.

Teresa resented the attention lavished on Matthew; she wanted Phil to spend time with her and Danny. Phil avoided handling the baby. "I love him, but he's so tiny."

She wanted Phil for herself and the baby, not Margaret and her son. "A baby needs a father. You're leaving me all the responsibility. It's not fair. Danny also needs you."

*   *   *

Danny celebrated his fifth birthday and Matthew, now seven . . . , started school. Five years passed and Phil had reneged on the vasectomy—he still was not ready. He let Teresa deal with the danger of another pregnancy, which stinted their sex life. Contrary to popular opinion, Teresa's memory of childbirth remained fresh in her mind. She held firm in her resolve never to bear another child.

Phil's obligation to pay child support to Margaret aggravated Teresa. *If I convince Matthew to live with us, Danny would have a companion and Phil wouldn't want more children.* Stealing Margaret's husband didn't satisfy her, she wanted Margaret's child. Through the years, the court increased the child support as Phil's finances prospered and Teresa begrudged every payment. *With full custody of Matthew Phil would not be obligated to pay Margaret. If Matthew lived with us, Phil would not have the responsibility to maintain Margaret's house. All that money would be ours.* When Matthew visited, Teresa urged him to live with them permanently. She showed him the school, the park playgrounds, the swimming pool, the library and the church. She stressed the companionship of his brother, Danny.

Phil unknowingly participated in her scheme. He'd take the boys to the park and fly their carefully constructed kites. Phil loved to build from kits; motorized remote controlled model planes and working rockets that they launched from a secluded beach. The child in him surfaced when with his children and he found welcome relief from the pressures of his job and Teresa's constant nagging to contact his lawyer. As usual, Teresa won. Phil sued Margaret for full custody of Matthew.

Margaret, distraught when notified by Phil's attorney about the custody hearing, phoned Ann Shelby. *Why did Phil and Teresa want to take him? Sure, my job keeps me busy and I occasionally travel out of New York, but these incidents are infrequent. I never neglected Matthew.*

Phil came to take Matthew for the weekend. Angry, Margaret said, "How can you disrupt Matthew's life? Can't you see he's happy?"

Phil hesitant—apologetic and under pressure answered, "Teresa and I feel that Matthew should grow up with the companionship of his brother."

"Would you give up Danny?"

"I know how you feel, but I believe the move is best for Matthew."

"I will not allow it!"

"You'll have him under the same conditions that I see him now."

"No! He's my child! No judge is going to take him from me."

"The Court date is set for September 12th. Let the judge decide what's best for Matthew."

Margaret bristled at Phil's audacity, inferring that she is an unfit mother. Their usual amicable feelings whenever they discussed Matthew changed into hatred.

"How could I have married you?"

"You wouldn't have Matthew if you didn't. Is he ready? I'll have him back Sunday evening about six. OK?"

Margaret hid her feelings from Matthew as he cheerfully left with his father.

"What's wrong with Mom?"

"Nothing. How would you and Danny like to go to the beach and fly our kites?"

"Yeah!"

Margaret's heart ached with fear of losing her son.

The breeze at the beach was unusually light, and Phil had difficulty keeping up with the boy's unsuccessful attempts to get their kites airborne. The loose sand made walking difficult. Before they reached the ocean's edge, where the water packed the sand hard as cement, Phil rested. He felt old, watching the children skitter over the sand; each boy wanted his kite to fly first and highest. Sudden fatigue overcame Phil; he always joined in their games. *I need my annual physical checkup.*

*   *   *

Monday morning, Phil arrived at his office, tired from the weekend with the boys. In the restroom, he washed his hands. The pallor of his fingernails bothered him; their healthy pink disappeared. He didn't feel right. Back at his desk, he phoned Doctor Revelli's office for an appointment. The receptionist asked, "Will Wednesday afternoon be convenient?

"Can the doctor see me earlier than Wednesday?"

"Is it an emergency?"

"Not really."

"Then he'll see you Wednesday."

Phil regretted his procrastination. The intervening day Phil tired easily. His complexion changed after the windburn from the beach wore off. In the afternoon, he dozed at his desk.

*   *   *

He stepped off the scale; the nurse noted his weight. She instructed him to strip to the waist and lie down, and then she attached the wires for an electrocardiogram. After discarding a test strip, she recorded a two-foot length and placed it in his folder. Phil winced as she filled three vials with his blood; it looked dark enough. She escorted him for a chest X-ray and then back to the examination room. Phil waited, listening to the all-pervasive music from a scratchy loudspeaker embedded in the ceiling. The buttons on the wall phone flashed; he made mental bets on which would light up next. The doctor may be busy, but for the patient, waiting feels interminable. Finally, the doctor appeared. "Phil, how are you feeling?"

"You tell me."

After checking the electrocardiogram he examined Phil with the stethoscope and sphygmomanometer. "No change in your ECG. Lungs clear—blood pressure is good."

Dr. Revelli examined both palms and his fingernails. After looking into Phil's eyes, he summoned the nurse and requested her to expedite the blood test.

When Doctor Revelli put the disposable rubber glove on his right hand, Phil shuddered, recalling memories of his last digital rectal examination.

"Drop your pants and bend over legs spread."

Dr. Revelli probed for the prostate.

". . . normal for your age." With a deft motion, the doctor removed the glove and deposited it in a red plastic receptacle.

". . . no blood in your stool. Call me Friday for your blood test results. You can dress."

He left the examining room without elaborating on Phil's general health.

On Friday Doctor Revelli phoned. "Phil—I received the results of your blood test. The numbers are out of line. Your white cell count is elevated indicating severe anemia. That accounts for your fatigue. I've called the hospital and requested a complete blood test and a bone marrow biopsy."

"Why bone marrow?"

"To determine the cause of diminishing red blood cells."

"Is it serious?" *Doctor Revelli would not have called otherwise.*

"I'll tell more after a comprehensive test."

*   *   *

Phil left for the hospital. *No need to alarm Teresa about the bone marrow biopsy until I get the results. With luck, depending on the hospital's proficiency, I'll be home at my regular time without arousing Teresa's fears.*

Chapter 20

Fate disrupted Teresa's idyllic married life. Phil's unexpected bout with leukemia was completely contrary to her plans. She wasn't into this sickness thing at all. Chemotherapy with multiple anticancer drugs and radiation treatments reduced Phil to a shell of his former self. Shaving his shiny bald scalp was no longer necessary and his face lacked eyebrows. The search for a bone marrow donor took longer than expected. With his immune system weakened, the doctor permitted only the closest relatives to visit. Teresa took this opportunity to gain an advantage for herself by telling Phil "I'm the only one that cares for you. No one comes to see you." Meanwhile she told everyone, including his mother and brother to stay away . . . a precaution against infection.

Angry at the judge's ruling against full custody of Matthew, Teresa disowned him—he was Phil's child and not hers. She stopped paying premiums on the term life insurance required to provide for Matthew's college education per the divorce agreement. Then she convinced Phil to write a new will and leave everything to her. "Trust me to care for Matthew and Danny. I'll raise them as brothers and never separate them." Phil, too ill to challenge her wishes, signed a new will witnessed by two hospital employees.

*   *   *

Upon release from the hospital, Phil returned home. Teresa always avoided sick people. Now necessity forced her to convert the living room of her Merrick home into a virtual hospital.

At the head of the adjustable bed, a white cabinet held medical necessities and in the far corner of the room, a cardboard carton stored clean linens. A mobile eating tray completed the hospital environment.

From the bed, Phil viewed the street through the front picture window or watched television. She replaced sheer curtains with opaque drapes to close for privacy. After witnessing the effects of chemotherapy in the hospital—the cold sweats accompanied by tremors and occasional vomiting—Teresa had an aversion to share her bed with him. After the leukemia diagnosis, she treated him as though the cancer was contagious, despite the oncologist's assurance to the contrary. She prepared the living room with concern for his comfort—she told him.

*   *   *

While the search for a suitable bone marrow donor continued, Phil underwent full body radiation and chemotherapy that required occasional hospitalization. His condition worsened and the doctor admitted him for observation. Travel to and from Manhattan would have been difficult for Teresa except for Mister Veidell's generosity that exceeded her expectations. Phil's boss arranged for use of the company suite—the same rooms that she shared with Phil during their extended lunch hours—rooms that triggered pleasant erotic memories.

Lying in bed, she missed him terribly and frustrated by the memory of their lovemaking, pounded the pillow with her fists. She pictured him, as he had been, not in his present weakened ravaged state. *He isn't the same man!* She cried herself to sleep, knowing the next day would bring more of the same. She was angry at Phil's leukemia and his 50-50 chance of survival. She had all she wished for—marriage, security, a home and the love of her child. Now she feared losing Phil.

*   *   *

After a day at the hospital, she entered the hotel's lounge and to relax, ordered wine. Aware of admiring glances in her direction, she was tempted encourage male companionship with a look or a smile, but when she thought of Phil's suffering, her needs could not compare. A man, apparently a visiting executive, with dark curly hair, light blue eyes and tanned complexion, slightly weathered and the promise of muscular arms under his tailored gray jacket impressed her.

One evening returning to the hotel after tending to Phil, she saw the handsome stranger with a red-haired woman wearing a miniskirt. He showed a badge and identified himself as Police Officer. The woman turned to run but he grasped her arm and held her until a uniformed officer arrived in a van. The woman cursed the detective as he hustled her into the van to join other vociferous prostitutes. *That could have been me!*

* * *

After spending the day at the hospital, she entered her room at the Helmsley™. Seated in front of the mirror, an attractive woman removed makeup. She asked, "Who are you? What are you doing here?"

"Hi! I'm Beverly. You must be Teresa." Her melodious voice with its rich North Carolinian accent surprised Teresa.

"Do I know you?"

"Veidell didn't tell you? I'm in town on business and he said you probably wouldn't mind sharing the suite."

The light on the phone indicated a message. Teresa dialed the front desk and asked, "Are there any messages?"

The clerk gave her the phone number of Phil's supervisor. It was late, so she assumed the call provided information about her roommate.

"Thanks to Mister Veidell's generosity, I have this suite close to the hospital. I welcome your company. My husband is at Sloan-Kettering™ for treatment."

"His name is Phil, isn't it?"

"Do you know him?"

"I met Mister Noble once, at a meeting in Charlotte, North Carolina. Together, we selected office furnishings for Veidell. I am truly sorry for his illness."

"I'll know more after the bone marrow transplant."

"You poor dear! I can't possibly know your anxiety. You're a remarkable woman. I envy your strength."

Beverly had a striking resemblance to Margaret, except for her light blond hair and slate blue eyes. Her complexion revealed traces of freckles. Her lips, pink even without lipstick, were full and sensuous. Her direct friendly manner indicated no guile regarding her acquaintance with Phil.

Phil meeting alone with this woman, business or otherwise filled Teresa's jealous mind. *Why didn't Phil ever mention Beverly? Perhaps, he had a reason.* Having experienced first-hand knowledge of his weakness for women, she knew Phil could easily be tempted. Now she wanted to say, "He can drop dead!" but after finding nothing but compassion in Beverly's eyes, dismissed the hideous thought of Phil's possible infidelity. When Beverly sympathized with Teresa rather than Phil, any obstacles to their friendship disappeared.

"I'm glad you're here. I needed someone to confide in." Teresa never had a woman friend, until now she considered all females as adversaries.

In the morning, they dressed and ate breakfast at a nearby coffee shop. Beverly accompanied Teresa to Sloan-Kettering™.

"He'll be surprised to see you. None of his work acquaintances ever visit." She wanted to see his reaction. Although she knew from Beverly that no romantic interest existed, she relished hearing Phil's version . . . why he never told her. *For an accomplished liar, that should be easy.*

*   *   *

Beverly could not believe this sallow, bald, shadow of a man was the same she met in North Carolina—the man who tempted her to break her rule to never mix business with her personal life. At his bedside, she extended her hand. "Hi Mister Noble. By a strange coincidence Teresa and I are room mates."

"Good to see you again, Beverly."

With eyes wide, over-sized for his drawn face, Phil touched her outstretched hand with an electrical reaction. *How much of our meeting did she tell Teresa? Did she give Teresa any inkling of my failure to seduce her? I can only hope.*

"Did you sleep well? Beverly told me you met in Charlotte. You never mentioned her"

"I leave my work at work; at home I'd rather speak of other matters."

His weak blood attempted to bring a flush to his face. Although pleased to see Beverly, he feared his cancer-ravaged condition created a hideous impression.

After three days as roommates, Beverly left for another assignment. Teresa missed her ready smile and upbeat attitude. Encouraged by Beverly's optimism, she hurried to Phil's side before the transplant scheduled that morning. With the harrowing search for a suitable donor over, Phil's survival now depended on the compatibility of a stranger's bone marrow.

Phil lay motionless in the hospital bed, grateful to the person who gave him a chance to live. Teresa held his hand and encouraged him. "You're strong. The new bone marrow will work. Danny and I both love you. He keeps asking when you're coming home."

Teresa waited for Phil to recover sufficiently before confronting him about his acquaintance with Beverly. She suspected his silence on the matter was deliberate. *He cheated on Margaret—would he cheat on me?*

A week after the transplant, she surprised him. "Did you share a room with her?"

"Who? What are you talking about? What room?"

". . . in North Carolina. I saw the charges on your credit card statement. That was where you met Beverly—wasn't it?"

". . . on business."

"Did she enter your room?"

"Only to freshen up after a tour of the dusty furniture showrooms. She wanted to wash before dinner."

"Oh! You had dinner together?"

"Yes, we had a business dinner together. What's wrong with that?"

"And you never once made a pass at her?"

"I admit I was tempted. I never thought of her that way. She's a business colleague."

He recalled the fleeting glimpse of Beverly's undulating body as the towel fell when she broke free of his grasp and ran into the bathroom. The chances of his wife rooming with a woman that he propositioned were phenomenally slim—and yet it happened. In his weakened condition, he prayed Teresa would leave him alone and end this inquisition.

Teresa sensed his annoyance. She had a gut feeling that Beverly had no designs on Phil but his pique encouraged her to continue her taunts.

"Did you have sex with her?"

"Are you crazy? Is that what she told you? I never touched her!"

A tinge of color rushed to his face with his denials. She toyed with him like a cat with a mouse. They had not argued since she learned of his leukemia; she enjoyed his discomfort.

"You know I love only you. My illness prevents me from showing you how much. If I could, I'd make love to you here and now." He slapped the mattress with the palm of his hand.

"I believe you. Get well so we can go home. I love you too." *Will our sexual passion ever return?*

* * *

He slowly regained strength. Dark fuzz appeared on his scalp signaling a new growth of hair. Outdoors, he wore a blue baseball cap to protect his head from sunburn.

The first weekend home, he, Danny and Matthew walked toward the swings in the playground.

"You don't know how much I missed you boys."

"I missed you, too." Matthew replied.

"And I missed you." Danny echoed.

"We all missed each other. Right?"

Phil grabbed both boys in a group hug. "I'm not going anywhere again. I promise. It's the three of us from now on."

* * *

Phil hated sleeping alone in the hospital bed that Teresa had set up for his care in the living room. "I despise this hospital bed. I don't need it. I think I'm well enough to move back into our bed.

"I'm only thinking of your comfort."

Teresa was reluctant to have him sleep beside her. He seemed a changed man with his gaunt limbs and fuzz for hair. It would be strange to feel him next to her. "But that bed is adjustable."

"The truth is that I miss you."

"I miss you too, darling. Perhaps we can try it for a night and see if you can get a restful sleep."

"I don't want the bed for only a night! Don't you want me back?"

"I do. Really . . . ." Since his health improved she had no other option.

* * *

Teresa managed the family finances as she had during his hospitalization. Freed from this burden, Phil lived life to the fullest . . . *best that she takes charge. If my cancer recurs, that would be her responsibility* He developed a compassion for his fellow patients and desired to help, especially the cancer-stricken children that life treated unfairly. On his scheduled checkup days, he brought books, toys and games to the hospital. He read stories to groups of children and played games with the bedridden. His lack of hair conformed to theirs; sometimes he wrapped a colorful scarf on his fuzzy head. On these days, Teresa accompanied him but never joined in the activities.

Fear of contracting a viral or bacterial infection prevented Phil from continuing his volunteer duties at the soup kitchen for the poor and homeless. The doctor warned that with his weakened immune system, he should avoid unnecessary exposure. Aware of his precarious condition, Phil attended Sunday Mass with Teresa and Danny after ignoring his faith for decades.

Fellow employees greeted him with a 'Welcome Back' party. His recovery changed his personality from a driving ambitious man willing to succeed at the expense of others—to a tolerant, helpful and cooperative person. He willingly assumed the role of mentor to promising recent hires that exhibited ambition and dedication.

Phil enjoyed his work. Now that Teresa handled the finances, he rarely glanced at his paycheck before endorsing it. He surrendered complete control. He viewed his victory over leukemia as temporary and found tranquility by living each day to its fullest.

* * *

Teresa always thought of Phil as a means to an end; now the change in him had an effect on her. Although the mother of Danny, mistress of her own home and with money, she lacked something within—she never loved Phil with her entire being—as soul mates. Her body performed the physical act of love but there never was a spiritual merging. Phil's attitude toward life changed and as days passed, he became more of a stranger.

She recalled the past—how she stole him from Margaret with help from Mama Louise, the weird woman who changed her destiny. The pittance she paid Mama Louise was little down payment for the wealth she now enjoyed. However, a sense of impending misfortune brought on tormenting nightmares.

In a dream, she found herself underground on a New York City subway train. People moved away from her, disgusted at the filthy dress she wore and her body odor. She had no place, no one—she was alone in life. She looked in her purse for money and found the leather pouch that Mama Louise had given her. It was empty with a slight residue coating the inside. *Could I have held on to Phil's love without her love charm?* The train rounded a curve in the track and the door between cars slid open. She shrieked as Mama Louise stood in the open doorway, dressed in colorful garb and ornaments that Teresa had last seen in apartment 6D. Fixing her with a penetrating stare, the mambo strained her raspy voice over the sounds of the speeding train, "Your luck has run out. Soon no one will love you. Your riches will not bring happiness. Outwardly you appear the fine lady; inwardly you are the wretch I see before me." A sudden lurch of the train and Mama Louise was gone. Teresa woke up screaming.

She felt Phil's arms around her; his soothing voice consoled her. "Teres' you had a nightmare. You're trembling. It must have been horrible."

"Don't let me go! I need you."

"What did you dream about?"

"I can't recall. But it was terrible. Hold me." *I cannot reveal the horror of my dream.*

Held close in Phil's comforting arms, she tried to banish thoughts of Mama Louise. Fearful of the nightmare recurring, she fell into a restless sleep.

Chapter 21

During Phil's period of treatment, Margaret, trying not to frighten the child, explained his father's ordeal to Matthew. "Don't expect your father to do all the things you did together before he got sick. He may feel weak and tire easily so I'd like both you and Danny to consider him before you make demands."

"Is daddy going to die?"

"The doctors are doing all they can so that won't happen."

"When I grow up I want to be a doctor and then I'll take care of him."

"You keep thinking that way and I'll help you. But you must study hard in school and get good grades."

"I will. I promise. Then I'll fix the sickness that made him go to the hospital."

Margaret beamed with pride. Inheriting her determination and his father's intellect, her boy will succeed.

She recently experienced all the symptoms of pregnancy but delayed telling David until she was sure. Near Christmas she surprised him with the news. David was ecstatic. Although he raised Matthew from infancy, he looked forward to the new experience of fathering his own child. "What a fantastic Christmas present—in my case Chanukah!"

*   *   *

Margaret's car slid on the treacherous ice hidden under a coating of fresh snow. She thought of Matthew's eagerness to rush outside and play with the children bundled against the cold; how they pelted each other with snowballs while they waited on the corner for the school bus—Matthew the most aggressive. If the snow continues, she would postpone shopping. She drove into the recently cleared executive parking area and unable to see the markings, estimated the location of her assigned spot. The force of the wind wrested the car door from her hand and snowflakes landed on the front seat. The swirling snow coated her in white. In the warmth of the lobby, she brushed off the melting flakes and cautiously walked on the slick wet marble floor to her office.

Inside, she draped her coat on a chair to dry near the air vent, and then paused at the window to admire the beauty of the scene. The snow-laden trees, shrubs and the expansive lawn covered by a white mantle bore little resemblance to her accustomed view. Henry, her assistant, carrying a steaming cup of hot chocolate, disrupted her thoughts. "This will warm you up! Relax. You have no appointments this morning. I have taken care of your mail. Enjoy the view."

"Thanks, Henry. You hover over me like a mother hen."

". . . my pleasure.

On her desk, the New York Times waited for her perusal—one of the perquisites given company executives to keep them abreast of the business world and current events. She skimmed over the articles; her eyes wandered to the large snowflakes, cotton puffs now that the wind subsided. She put the paper down and surrendered to the serenity of the view.

Henry startled her. "Mister Burns invited you to lunch, today. I told him you would join him."

Regaining her composure, she said, "Thank you, Henry. I could not refuse Ted since he hired me. Could I?" *Why did Ted Burns arrange to meet with me personally?*

* * *

Ted's distinguished appearance, improved with age. "Margaret, you are more beautiful every day. It's a shame that it snowed on the day I planned our luncheon."

"There's always the company cafeteria."

"Don't think of it. This day is special. The cafeteria is too noisy for conversation. There are excellent restaurants within walking distance—if you don't mind the snow."

"I love snow. I had fun in my childhood, lying in the snow and making the outline of an angel by sweeping my arms."

"And I used to write my initials. Please, don't expect me to demonstrate."

They walked arm-in-arm to the luncheonette, until Ted Burns slipped and landed on the icy sidewalk. He almost pulled Margaret down with him. Margaret attempted to help him, but Ted refused assistance. Awkwardly rising from the pavement, he limped attempting to conceal his pain with a feeble laugh. As they entered the luncheonette, Margaret asked, "Do you think you'll be comfortable sitting after that fall?"

Ignoring her question, his pride hurt more than his rear, Ted led her to a table with a red-checkered tablecloth and an unidentifiable artificial flower in a slim milk-glass vase. After taking their order, the waiter brought hot coffee for Ted and decaffeinated tea for Margaret. The cozy atmosphere blended with odor of home cooking gave their meeting a sense of intimacy.

Ted spoke first. "I'll come to the point. The Board of Directors asked me to nominate a candidate for Vice President of Marketing. I submitted your name."

"I'm flattered that you considered me. Normally, I wouldn't hesitate; however, you might change your mind."

"You have doubts? I'm certain you'll do an excellent job."

"I'd love the job, but truthfully I'm pregnant."

"Then you'll be our first pregnant vice-president. As the founder of our company day care center, you can do quality control and improve its operation through practical experience."

"You still want me in the job? I wouldn't embarrass you for sponsoring me when I attend meetings with a distended belly?"

"I'll tell the Board members that pregnant or not, you're qualified."

"With your support, I shall manage. Thanks for your confidence. I accept the nomination."

She sealed their pact with a firm handshake.

The waiter served Margaret's salad and Ted's sandwich piled high with lean roast beef. "This looks good." Would you like to trade? You need nourishment for two—I don't."

*　　*　　*

Three weeks prior her due date, Margaret arranged for maternity leave. On her last workday, the staff decorated her desk and office for a surprise baby shower. Her car could not hold all the gifts so Henry loaded the presents in his van and followed her home. He forbade her to carry anything and set the gifts down in the nursery.

"Would you like a cup of coffee?" Margaret offered.

"No, thank you. I'm admiring what you've done with this room—everything beautifully color-coordinated and planned for efficiency. You're tired after a hectic day. Call me when the baby arrives. Don't forget!"

"Drive safely—thanks again."

*　　*　　*

On July 25, Margaret, with David at her side in the delivery room gave birth to a girl, Ariel Jean. Mathew welcomed the baby with mixed emotions. After years as the center of his mother's love, he had mixed feelings sharing her with this newcomer. The happy visitors that filled the bustling hospital corridors, peered through the nursery windows, waved and called to the newborn changed his mood. David lifted him and Matthew was amazed at the rows of babies, with their pink or blue identification tags.

"Which one is ours?"

"I don't see her. Maybe your mother has her. She's in room 312."

They found Margaret sitting in bed and cuddling the baby. David remarked on her appearance. "You'd make a beautiful portrait."

"Matthew, meet your little sister."

Awed and slightly jealous, Matthew replied, "Mom, I miss you. When are you coming home?"

"When the doctor tells me that I can. Her name is Ariel Jean. Aren't you going to say 'Hello' to her?"

"Can I touch her?"

"Sure you can. She won't break."

She grasped his finger. "She's strong! Look—she has my finger. When can she come home?"

"Soon. Then you can play with her all day."

"But she can't do anything."

"You'll teach her. You're her big brother now."

"I'm the big brother?"

"Yes, you are . . . ."

When they left, Margaret guided the baby to her breast. The sensation induced serenity reminiscent of the first time she nursed Matthew. She found security in the love and support of her husband and son—in sharp contrast to the circumstances surrounding Matthew's birth.

*   *   *

At that time, her emotions were in turmoil. She knew of Phil's affair but for the sake of her child forgave him; she had little faith in his promises. Later she discovered that Teresa waited in the hospital lobby while Phil attended Matthew's birth in the delivery room. He drove home with Teresa and slept with her within sight of the waiting nursery.

Margaret pictured Phil doing things in her bed that were their own private secrets. *What entered his mind? Were his thoughts the same he had with me or did his guilt add to the excitement? They showered together! Teresa used my perfume and toiletries. She replaced me in Phil's life. He missed afternoon visiting hours—he was exhausted and fell asleep. He plied me with lies and promises then created a big fuss over fatherhood—kissed the baby and me—told me he loved me while Teresa waited downstairs.*

*   *   *

After their divorce, Phil prompt with child support payments, visited Matthew regularly but David spent more time with Matthew. David treated the boy like his son. David put the Band-Aid® on his scratched knee after a fall. David taught him to swim; gave him confidence and encouragement. However, Margaret still harbored feelings toward Phil despite his treatment of her. Extremely happy after giving birth to Ariel Jean, she could not help feeling sad at Phil's admission to Sloan-Kettering™ when his leukemia relapsed.

She last saw him at Matthew's Confirmation at the Sacred Heart Church. At that time, he had undergone chemotherapy and his hair returned as dark black fuzz. Despite the hair loss, he appeared gaunt but handsome. With his eyes on Margaret, he tried to pass Margaret's mother seated at the end of the pew. "Is it OK to sit next to that beautiful woman?"

"It is not! She's no longer your wife." mother replied while moving over to make room for Phil.

He reached out his hand to congratulate David. "I'm surprised to see you in a Catholic church."

"I respect Margaret's religion and she respects mine. We're proud of Matthew and will always be there for him."

"As will I—at least until this cancer finishes me."

Now Phil lies in a struggle for survival, combating pneumonia while she holds a new life in her arms. With a prayer, she forgave his cruelty toward her and wished him well. She blamed Teresa and could never forgive her. Finding happiness now with David, Matthew, and Ariel, changed Margaret's life forever.

Chapter 22

Phil's relapse of leukemia put him back in the hospital. Teresa held an all night vigil at his bedside. The wheeze of the respirator and beeps of the heart monitor broke the silence in the Intensive Care Unit. He lie motionless with his eyes closed apparently unaware of her presence. Teresa watched as he struggled to breathe through plastic tubes in his nostrils. She took his hand in hers and softly spoke, "Phil, I'm here. You have to fight. Danny and I love you. We need you!" She felt him squeeze her hand and saw the fear in his eyes as he opened them momentarily.

Erratic beeps from the heart monitor formed a continuous tone. Alarms at the nurse's station triggered a flurry of activity; a doctor and nurse rushed in with a defibrillator and attempted to resuscitate Phil while Teresa, in shock, watched. The nurse shouted for her to leave while they worked over Phil's inert body. After several minutes of futile effort, the doctor approached Teresa. "I'm sorry. His immune system weakened by chemotherapy failed to overcome the complication of pneumonia. Go to him, if you wish."

With the life sustaining equipment removed, Phil appeared an emaciated old man. *This isn't the vibrant Phil I know, the father of my child!* She made the sign of the cross and whispered a prayer asking God to forgive his sins and welcome his soul into heaven and then placed a farewell kiss on his brow. She briefly examined her conscience and decided she had time for atonement.

Twice-widowed before reaching the age of thirty-two Teresa thought, *do I indeed posed a threat to any man I marry; Frank in his thirties killed by a car and now Phil at forty-two by leukemia, both comparatively young men in the prime of life. Am I destined to follow the pattern set by my aunt and mother . . . to live my life a lonely widow?*

*   *   *

The October sun accentuated the whitecaps covering the ocean's blue water and fine sand particles carried by a brisk breeze pelted Teresa's face. Danny and Matthew laughed at the raucous sea gulls fighting over a hot dog roll that Danny dropped. Teresa cradled the urn containing Phil's ashes in her arms. She explained to the boys "Daddy loved Jones Beach and wanted his ashes scattered over the water." At the waters edge she removed the cover. Matthew always inquisitive asked, "Can I see?"

Danny chimed in, "Me too."

"Are you sure you want to . . ."

Together they answered, "Yes, we're sure."

Matthew looked in the urn—disappointed.

"That's not Daddy. It's dirt."

"Teresa explained to the confused boys that ashes remained after cremation; but they lost interest and returned to chasing sea gulls.

She walked ankle-deep into the surf, raised the urn in both hands and scattered the ashes over the water. "Good-bye Phil. I'm fulfilling your wishes." Then she placed the open urn on its side in the path of an incoming wave. The ocean water washed out the residue and Phil became one with the sea.

Teresa called to the children "Danny and Matthew, how would you like an ice cream cone?" In response and with youthful energy they circled her as she walked through the loose sand toward the concession area. The gravity of their mission completely escaped them. Teresa carried the empty urn in a plastic shopping bag. *Why didn't I throw it in the water? Whatever do people do with them after they served their purpose?*

Chapter 23

Phil made many new friends during his leukemia remission. At their request, Teresa arranged a memorial service at the parish of his volunteer activity. Grateful for Phil's help organizing church projects, the pastor insisted on conducting the service. On Sunday, he invited everyone touched by Phil's life to attend.

In the front pew, the grieving widow in a black silk dress and wide-brimmed hat peered through a fine mesh veil. Danny and Matthew fidgeted in their black suits, frequently loosening the collars of their white starched shirts, made tighter by the unaccustomed long black neckties. White sneakers sharply contrasted their somber appearance; they had outgrown their shoes. Eric and Phil's mother unsuccessfully tried to keep Matthew and Danny quiet as the boys poked and taunted each other.

The turnout surprised Margaret and David, unaware of Phil's popularity with the parishioners. Margaret's parents, seated alongside her, attended in respect for their grandson's father. An occasional cough or the sound of a kneeler hitting the hard floor echoed throughout the otherwise silent church.

The sound of bells signaled the start of the services as the pastor, wearing a black chasuble over his white alb and black cassock entered the sanctuary preceded by two acolytes; concealing cassocks and surplices prevented positive gender determination. With both servers wearing long hairstyles, the congregation could only surmise.

Standing behind the altar railing, the priest opened with prayers for the welfare of Phil's soul. He spoke of Phil helping the unfortunate and his talent organizing parishioner participation. He praised Phil's exemplary life and love of family. Then his narrative faltered at the sight of one incongruent member of the congregation, a wrinkled dark-skinned woman. She wore a multicolored scarf formed into a turban, strings of beads around her neck and bracelets on both arms. Her flowing garment contained the colors of the rainbow. The contrast, inappropriate for the solemnity of the occasion isolated her from other mourners.

Teresa aware of the pastor's distraction turned her head to determine the cause. Sudden recognition startled her. *How did Mama Louise find out about the memorial service? True, she concocted the love potion that precipitated Phil's divorce. Why is she here? Does she want to share the insurance money? If she doesn't bother me, I won't bother her.*

The priest called on Phil's brother, Eric. Although close during childhood, after puberty Eric and his brother pursued different interests. Goal-oriented Phil excelled in business while Eric followed a career in public service. He cleared his throat, "My brother, Phil didn't deserve the ravages of leukemia and the effects of chemotherapy and radiation. He fought for survival but succumbed in the prime of life. Phil generously offered help to the needy and we can benefit from his example. He loved his family, taking special delight in his sons. Matthew and Danny, cherish the memories of hours building model rockets, flying ingenious kites and visits to Jones Beach."

Matthew heard his name and whispered to Teresa "Uncle Eric is talking about daddy and me." She motioned for silence with a finger to her lips as Eric continued. "Phil, we miss you!" Eric's voice faltered.

Eric failed to include Teresa or Margaret in the eulogy. Margaret wondered if it was intentional. *How much did Eric know of Phil's infidelity before the divorce and his marriage to Teresa? Phil must have confided in him.*

The pastor concluded the service with a blessing and invoked God to welcome Phil's soul into heaven.

The memorial service was unlike any she ever attended—Phil's ashes had already been scattered in the ocean. Margaret impulsively tended to forgive Phil for the pain he caused and offer sympathy to the widow but Teresa avoided glancing in her direction. Instead, Margaret went to Matthew, and with a hug and a kiss said, "Be a good boy and mind Teresa. She'll bring you home on Monday." Then Margaret and David offered condolences to Eric and commented on his touching eulogy. The boys followed Teresa to her car and dutifully buckled seat belts before she started the engine. Danny sat in the front seat ready to defend his rights if Matthew challenged him. Matthew sat quietly in the rear. Teresa broke the silence, "You boys must be starved. How would you like a Happy Meal® at McDonald™?" With a resounding "Yes!" their sad faces immediately brightened.

*   *   *

Despite Teresa's promise to raise the boys together, Mathew drifted away, as did Phil's ashes in the waves at Jones Beach. Her life centered upon Danny, enrolling him in private school. After probating Phil's will and upon her lawyer's advice, she grudgingly set up an account for $50,000 under control of Phil's mother to fulfill the terms of his divorce that covered Matthew's education. She bought a new Mustang™ convertible and entered Hofstra University™. Teresa's dreams of security, home, a child, and marriage had come true—except for losing the man she loved. With a comfortable income from Phil's life insurance and Veidell's benefits, Teresa no longer needed a job. She dwelled upon keeping her physical appearance youthful with exercise and beauty care. She attracted men and had no problem forming relationships, but when they hinted at marriage, she promptly avoided commitment.

She feared that any man married to her was destined for an early death. She had everything—except love.

###

Printed in the United States
68660LVS00003B/178-186

9 781425 747374